EDITORS
Susan Burmeister-Brown   Linda Burmeister Davies

CONSULTING EDITORS
Charles Asher   Kimberly Bennett
Brittney Corrigan-McElroy   Jennifer Jackson Reynolds
Roz Wais   Kris Wood

COPY EDITOR
Scott Allie

PROOFREADER
Rachel Penn

TYPESETTING & LAYOUT
Paul Morris

ADMINISTRATIVE ASSISTANTS
Kaylin Elaine Dodge   Erin Swanson-Davies

COVER ARTIST
Jane Zwinger

STORY ILLUSTRATOR
Jon Leon

PUBLISHED QUARTERLY
in spring, summer, fall, and winter by **Glimmer Train Press, Inc.**
710 SW Madison Street, Suite 504, Portland, Oregon 97205-2900
Telephone: 503/221-0836   Facsimile: 503/221-0837
www.glimmertrain.com

PRINTED IN U.S.A.
Indexed in *The American Humanities Index.*

Glimmer Train (ISSN #1055-7520), registered in U.S. Patent and Trademark Office, is published quarterly, $32 per year in the U.S., by Glimmer Train Press, Inc., Suite 504, 710 SW Madison, Portland, OR 97205. Periodicals postage paid at Portland, OR, and additional mailing offices. POSTMASTER: Send address changes to Glimmer Train Press, Inc., Suite 504, 710 SW Madison, Portland, OR 97205.

STATEMENT OF OWNERSHIP, MANAGEMENT, AND CIRCULATION. Required by 39 USC 3685, file date: 9/28/99. Publication name: Glimmer Train, publication #10557520. Published quarterly (4x/yr). Publisher and owner: Glimmer Train Press, Inc. Complete mailing address of known office of publication and headquarters is 710 SW Madison, #504, Portland, OR 97205-2900. One-year subscription price: $32. Editors and co-presidents: Susan Burmeister-Brown and Linda Burmeister Davies, 710 SW Madison, #504, Portland, OR 97205-2900. Known bondholders: none. Extent and nature of circulation: a) average number of copies each issue during preceding 12 months, b) actual number of copies of single issue published nearest to filing date. Net press run: a) eleven thousand, four hundred seventy-five; b) thirteen thousand, two hundred. Paid or requested mailed outside-county mail subscriptions: a) five thousand, seven hundred sixty-eight; b) six thousand, eight hundred seventy-four. Paid or requested mailed inside-county mail subscriptions: a) none; b) none; Sales through distributors: a) three thousand, four hundred eighty; b) three thousand, two hundred sixty. Other Classes: a) twenty; b) twenty. Total paid/requested circulation: a) nine thousand, two hundred sixty-eight; b) ten thousand, one hundred fifty-four. Free distribution outside-county by mail: a) one hundred; b) one hundred. Free distribution inside-county by mail: a) none; b) none. Free distribution, other classes: a) none; b) none. Free distribution outside of mail: a) two hundred forty; b) two hundred forty. Total free distribution: a) three hundred forty; b) three hundred forty. Total distribution: a) nine thousand, six hundred eight; b) ten thousand, four hundred ninety-four. Copies not distributed: a) one thousand, eight hundred sixty seven; b) two thousand, seven hundred six. Total sum of distributed and not distributed copies: a) eleven thousand, four hundred seventy-five; b) thirteen thousand, two hundred. Percent Paid and or Requested Circulation: a) ninety-six; b) ninety-six. I certify that the statements made by me above are correct and complete—Linda Burmeister Davies, Editor.

ISSN # 1055-7520, ISBN # 1-880966-32-8, CPDA BIPAD # 79021

DISTRIBUTION: Bookstores can purchase *Glimmer Train Stories* through these distributors:
               Ingram Periodicals, 1226 Heil Quaker Blvd., LaVergne, TN 37086
               IPD, 674 Via de la Valle, #204, Solana Beach, CA 92075
               Peribo PTY Ltd., 58 Beaumont Rd., Mt. Kuring-Gai, NSW 2080, AUSTRALIA
               Ubiquity, 607 Degraw St., Brooklyn, NY 11217
SUBSCRIPTION SVCS: EBSCO, Faxon, Readmore, Turner Subscriptions, Blackwell's UK

Subscription rates: One year, $32 within the U.S. (Visa/MC/check).
Airmail to Canada, $43; outside North America, $54.
Payable by Visa/MC or check for U.S. dollars drawn on a U.S. bank.

Attention short-story writers: We pay $500 for first publication and onetime anthology rights. Send manuscripts (with SASE) in January, April, July, and October. Send SASE for guidelines, or visit our website for information on our Short-Story Award for New Writers, our Very Short Fiction Award, and our Fiction and Poetry Opens.

*Glimmer Train Press also offers **Writers Ask**—nuts, bolts, and informed perspectives— a quarterly newsletter for the committed writer. One year, four issues, $20 within the U.S. ($26 beyond the U.S.), Visa, MC or check to Glimmer Train Press, Inc., or order online at www.glimmertrain.com.*

Dedication

We dedicate this issue to William Howard Salvesen,
born in Hinsdale, Illinois, on May 27, 1923, died in
Portland on September 30, 1999. Bill Salvesen waved
to us from his red leather chair in the Sovereign
Collection art gallery every morning.
Our office is upstairs in the same building, and when
we rode the slow elevator together, we could count
on a story, and we would laugh with him—not
to be polite to a sweet old man, which he was,
but because he was a terrific storyteller.
His sophistication and wit never failed, and
his good-natured dignity was always evident.
Things will not be the same without him.

As an aspiring writer,
year unknown.

As we knew him.

Photo credit: Mark Barnes, 1990

Susan & Linda

CONTENTS

$\mathscr{C}$ONTENTS

Robin Winick

*Believe it or not, in honor of my cousin's
wedding, my mother took me all the way to
Manhattan to have my hair cut like this! For
the next fifteen years, my father and I got our
hair cut together at the neighborhood barber.*

Robin Winick lives in Old Greenwich, Connecticut, with her husband,
Larry, and two daughters, Meryl and Carol. She has had a poem published
in *Lynx Eye* and a short story published in *Happy*, both of which have been
nominated for a Pushcart Prize this year.

ROBIN WINICK
Cosgrove's Dilemma

*J*he rain outside Herbert Cosgrove's window fell in vast translucent sheets, as if a dam somewhere up in the heavens had burst, unleashing a grand and final deluge. Oh, not forty days of rain, as in the Great Flood; no, that was in the old days when God had time on his hands, but now, today, in the breathtaking Modern Age, the flood would be instantaneous and relentless.

The sump pump had given out in the basement, and the water was rising, lapping at the bottom stair on the first floor, and simultaneously draining into the spongy earth, creating an expansive slough beneath the foundation of the house. Herbert Cosgrove had waited too long, and now his house was about to sink into a great morass.

Last year he had been caught in a down draft on an airplane, and the plane had started to plummet, just fall out of the sky and into the fathomless ocean. Even though it had leveled off, the sinking feeling had stayed with him, and no amount of rational explanation of the aerodynamics of flight made sense to him; so he had stopped flying, convinced that only a miracle could keep a plane in the air for an entire flight. Now the house was sinking because there was simply nothing that could hold it above the saturated earth. He looked out the window through the sheets of water and noticed his greenish brown lawn undulating, as if it were merely a thin mat above a vast subterranean sea, and figured his suburban square of land had evolved into a primordial quaking bog.

Well, why not? He had lost faith. The bottom was dropping out of everything, not just his house. Stocks plummeted, planes regularly fell out of the sky, computers crashed, information destabilized and vanished into the void of the monitor, his Aunt Lydia had vanished into nowhere on an exotic vacation, and a prodigious slab of throughway had plunged into the river a mile from his house, taking a truck and two cars along with it. The foundation of life was not just cracking, slowly, silently, without notice; it was disintegrating before his eyes.

The teeming rain and shimmering lawn made him feel dizzy and uprooted, but despite a local rumor of his lunacy, he knew of no such aberration. He had merely a unique perspective. The substance had disappeared from his life, leaving him with the feeling that the underlying basis of everything was simply nothing, a hollow core, and that the supposedly rational world was based on a senseless, timeless void. He argued with his dwindling group of friends that it wasn't so much that people were crazy but that the world was. In the face of their simplistic arguments to the contrary, he went so far as to say that insanity was an illusory state in which an individual perceives order, systems, and patterns where none exist.

Herbert Cosgrove made himself a cup of tea. He sat on his couch and sipped slowly, until he felt drowsy from its warmth and drifted into a light sleep, awakening shortly to a cacophony of sloshing, slapping, and sucking noises. The room had grown dark, as if dusk had descended early. He went to his window and peered out into the thick, murky weather. The lights in his neighborhood had been extinguished, though it was early, and he stared out over an immense gloom.

He leaped up the stairs, a feeling of disquietude creeping about him like a thickening fog, and looked through the second-floor window. The rain was falling in thick sheets, a veritable deluge; yet the gloom was not so abysmal as it was from the first-floor window. A faint light, filtering through the clouds, allowed Herbert the opportunity to notice his weedy, ill-kept lawn directly outside the second-story window. An unwelcomed thought seized hold of his mind: The murky gloom outside the first-floor windows must be a suspension of water and soil *below* his lawn. He had been right all along; and now he thought only of a tortuous death by suffocation.

He remembered his glasses were on the couch downstairs where he had napped. Fearfully, he descended the stairs, hesitating at intervals, feeling as if he were entering a dank, airless cavern. Once on the first floor, his nostrils filled with the musty odor of damp mud, and the next thing he sensed was his tongue feeling thick and heavy and coated. When he inhaled, he felt a lump at the base of his throat and a great heaviness in his chest, as if the air he inhaled was solidifying within him. Taking shallow breaths, he groped along the couch for his glasses, trying to resist the sensation of the walls closing in on him from the pressure of the slough swallowing the house. He lifted the pillows and threw them around, grasping, sticking his fingers in the cracks of the sofa and along the back until he found his glasses, then bounded up the stairs, his heart pounding so hard he thought it would burst through his chest cavity and crash at his feet.

He took a seat on the radiator in his bedroom and peered through the window. The lawn with its profusion of English plantain, dandelions, clover, and a vast array of unmanageable weeds—yes, his offensive lawn that roused the ire and indignation of his neighbors—had been transformed into a quavering field of floating sphagna, purple liverwort, sedge, and heather.

He pressed his glasses against the window pane and trained them on the house across the street. If he didn't know himself

so completely, he might actually suppose his mind were playing tricks on him. Through the sheets of translucent rain and the low, bulging clouds, he caught a glimpse of the Heusteds cooking dinner in one of those new fancy smokers. A shaft of brilliant sun danced on the roof of their home and lit up the hair of the children tumbling on the lawn. Mr. Johnson, down one house to the left, was mowing his lawn, and the Babcocks to the right were chatting, as if it were just another ordinary afternoon.

Not one of them looked across the street at his house enveloped in a dark, freakish weather pattern; not one of them noticed his house sinking into the earth, while they chatted about nothing, as usual. It was always like that. He was incensed.

The bog was rising, or the house was sinking; he was in such a state of confusion that he didn't know which, but half the second floor was below the level of the topsoil now. He had to get to the roof. He climbed the attic stairs, pried open the window, squeezed through, and clawed his way up the wet slippery shingles; then, straddling the roof peak, he inched his way toward the chimney and pulled himself up, hugging the brick outcropping for dear life.

"Hey, Johnson," he called out, but his voice was weak against the storm raging about him. "Hey, Heusted!" he shrieked, but neither Johnson nor Heusted answered. Mr. Johnson had the lawnmower going; the Heusteds were guzzling cocktails and peering hungrily into the smoker. And the Babcocks chatted away, occasionally eyeing Cosgrove's house and frowning, as if they noticed a shutter unhinged or his paint job chipping and peeling, or some other Cosgrovian assault on their sensibilities.

In the midst of his petty thoughts, maybe his last, he felt the house shift and then rock, slowly, ponderously, like an overburdened ferry. The house had become unhinged from the earth. Herbert locked his arms around the chimney and shut his eyes. A great force was at work, trying to yank him from the chimney. He embedded his nails in the brickwork and clutched the chimney, listening to his furniture crash against the interior walls of his house. He thought of the *Titanic* upending and sinking into the cold dark sea. The bog swelled and ebbed, lapping at the roof eaves, slapping and sucking, heaving and gurgling, as it greedily digested the house.

In all the tumult, Herbert looked about him and down at the loose suspension of mossy sphagna, mud, and water lapping at his feet. As if he were in the eye of a storm, the pitching and rocking ceased. The house was settling into the bog, as if it had consciously succumbed. He was not to be catapulted off the roof in some ungodly configuration of body parts and land upside down in the bog, nor was he to precipitously sink therein. His exit from the world would be, in a manner of speaking, almost deliberate. So as he stood on his roof, embracing his chimney, the bog about his waist sucking at his shirttail, he gazed upon the strange stormy darkness about him and the late-afternoon sun illuminating his neighbors, and determined he had the ultimate proof of his assumption that people were not crazy: situations were irrational.

VERY SHORT FICTION AWARD
1st-, 2nd-, and 3rd-Place Winners

First-place winner: ROBIN WINICK

Robin Winick receives $1200 for her first-place story, "Cosgrove's Dilemma," which begins on page 7, preceded by her profile on page 6.

Second-place winner: LEE UPTON

Lee Upton receives $500 for "The Worm Belongs to the Apple." A recipient of the National Poetry Series Award and the Pushcart Prize, she is the author of four books of poetry (including the award-winning Civilian Histories*), three books of criticism (most recently* The Must of Abandonment*), and her fiction has appeared in numerous literary publications.*

"The Worm Belongs to the Apple"

I was leaving slowly, maybe, but I would push out of every place I knew and take the impress of the larger world on my skin.

Third-place winner: J. ALICIA SHANK

J. Alicia Shank receives $300 for "Every Happy Family." She is twenty-two and has a BA from the University of Notre Dame, where she won the Richard T. Sullivan Award for fiction writing. Her fiction has appeared in the Michigan Quarterly Review. *She is currently paying for her MA in creative writing at the University of Colorado by writing rock criticism and tutoring football players.*

"Every Happy Family"

The uncles, their heads beery, their eyes a little wet, will idealize their estimations of each other, of their children, of their wives, and they will grab the aunts and kiss them with passion, being too old for concern over the embarrassment of youth.

We invite you to our website (www.glimmertrain.com) to see a listing of the top twenty-five winners and finalists. We thank all entrants for sending in their work.

James Carlos Blake

*At age seven, I was a proud Longhorn
living in Brownsville, Texas.*

James Carlos Blake was born in Mexico and raised in Texas and Florida. His novella "I, Fierro" won the 1991 Quarterly West Novella Competition, and his story "Under the Sierras" won the national Authors in the Park Short-Story Prize in 1993. In addition to the novels *The Pistoleer* (1995), *The Friends of Pancho Villa* (1996), *In the Rogue Blood* (winner of the *Los Angeles Times* Book Prize for Fiction in 1997), and *Red Grass River* (Avon Books, 1998), he has published a short-fiction collection, *Borderlands* (Avon Books, 1999). He lives in El Paso, Texas, and DeLand, Florida.

JAMES CARLOS BLAKE
Old Boys

loyd says he's through with hunting forever—
swears it—that's how bitter this whole thing's made him. The
rest of us just grin and take a swig of beer and say, "Yeah,
right." Not a man among us hasn't sworn off something or
other forever and then gone out and done it again. Not a man
among us hasn't done that more than once.

Besides, Floyd's not the only one with reason to be bitter.
Charlie's got at least as much reason as he does, but you don't
hear him saying he's through with hunting. Actually, nobody's
heard Charlie say anything since that last hunting trip, and it's
more than a week now. He's been staying home and refusing
to even come to the phone. His wife Hallie Anne tells whichever one of us happens to call that he still isn't saying very
much even to her. She says all he does is sit in front of the TV
and drink beer and bite her head off if she says boo. His
foreman's about out of patience with him and said if he
doesn't get his ass out to the work site pretty soon he's out of
a job. Zeller drove over to his house the other day and sat out
front honking the horn till Hallie Anne came out and told
him Charlie said if he didn't quit it he'd take a tire iron to his
truck. Yes sir, Charlie's plenty pissed off himself, but he's not
real sure exactly who he should be pissed off *at*, so he's staying

pissed at everybody. Just the same, he hasn't said he's through with hunting, not like Floyd.

But don't even mention Charlie to Floyd. "You ain't ever gonna see me out hunting again," Floyd said during happy hour at The Dog House the other day, "but you ever see me out hunting with *that* peckerwood again, you got my permission to shoot me and put my head on your wall."

Ira and me gave each other a look when he said that. We couldn't help but remember how close Carol came to shooting him when we got back from the hunt.

Carol's Floyd's wife. They've been fighting like cats and dogs since before they got married right out of high school. Fifteen years and two kids later and they're still going at it. Not too different from most married people, I guess, except they go at it with a little more fire than most couples.

You could say that Floyd's present unhappiness with hunting was caused by one of their fights. Whatever the argument was about that time, Floyd was in the right for a change, and to make it up to him Carol bought him a present. She's like that: hell in high heels whenever Floyd yanks her chain, but the rest of the time a whole lot sweeter to him than he probably deserves. Anyhow, what she bought him was a brand-new Winchester thirty-thirty carbine.

He told us about it at The Dog House during Monday Night Football, and at half-time we all went out to his truck to have a look at it. Charlie wanted to try it out right then and there. "I got ten bucks says I can shoot out that streetlight yonder," he said, pointing at a light two blocks away.

"You can shoot off your mouth is what you can shoot," Floyd said. "Nobody's firing this baby before I do, and the first shot I take with it I'm putting down a deer, you watch and see."

It was a fine-looking piece, all right, a dandy present to get two weeks before the start of hunting season. Or so we all thought.

The five of us have known each other just about all our lives, and we've been hunting together since back when we were in junior high school. We usually start to get ready a week or so before the opening day of the season. We oil the guns, stock up on food and whiskey, air out and re-pack the sleeping bags, and load up whichever two trucks we've decided to take. On the morning before opening day we head on out, and for the next few days the wives call us in sick at work. The bosses know what we're doing, but we're all damn good at our jobs, and as long as we don't miss more than three or four days they don't ever give us too much flack about it.

By mid-afternoon we'll be in the Big Cypress Swamp and setting up camp. By sunset we'll be cooking a good meal on the fire and having a few snorts with beer chasers to ease the whiskey burn. We'll stay up late that first night, drinking and telling stories around the fire while the darkness pulls in tighter all around us, and the trees seem to get taller and closer together. The air turns wet and heavy, and mist starts rising off the ponds. If there's any moon at all—but especially if the moon's full—the picture it makes through the trees is so beautiful you can't even describe it, you can only feel it in your throat. When we finally crawl into our sleeping bags, I always like to lie awake a while and listen to the swamp, to the frogs ringing in the ponds and the owls hooting in the trees, and every now and then some bull gator growling for a mate. One time I heard a panther cry out way off in the distance, I swear I did. Everybody called me a liar when I told them the next morning, but they were just jealous. Except for the oldtimers, it's not many anymore can say they've heard a panther in the wild.

Anyhow, the day before we set out this time, I was pumping iron in the rec room and dropped a ten-pound plate on my foot. Broke my big toe and one of the bones along the top. When my wife Brenda was driving me back from the emergency room I said I'd be damned if I wasn't going on the hunt anyway. She rolled her eyes in that way she knows I can't stand and said I was real likely to sneak up on a deer with a cast on my foot. She always gets extra-bitchy when the season comes around, like hunting was invented specifically to irritate her.

Naturally, the other guys all had a big laugh when they came by for me the next morning and saw the cast. Charlie said, "That's what you get for thinking you're man enough to kick Brenda's ass, Jake." Brenda was at the front door in her robe and gave a big snicker. Ha ha. Charlie's one to talk, the kind of wars he has with Hallie Anne. Just a couple of months ago they had a hellacious fight and she locked him out of the house. When he broke open the kitchen door, she was laying for him with a cast-iron skillet. Charlie's the biggest of us and has a head like concrete, but the way Hallie Anne told it to Brenda he went down like a killed man. She quick called 911 and pressed dishrags to his bloody scalp till the paramedics got there and took him to the hospital for stitches. As I got into Ira's truck I said that if I still had a humongous skillet scar on *my* head I sure wouldn't be too quick to make dumb jokes about anybody breaking his foot on his wife's ass.

Even in November South Florida can be a scorcher, but this year the weather was absolutely perfect: sunny but cool enough to be comfortable in a shooting jacket. The sky was cloudless, so deep and brightly blue it made you light in the head to stare up into it.

We drove out on Alligator Alley about thirty miles and then turned south into the swamp on an old limerock road that got rougher and narrower as it went along. About a half-hour later we came to an oystershell trail that branched eastward and was barely wide enough to accommodate a pickup. We had to go even slower now, the trucks bouncing and swaying as the trail went winding through prairie grass as high as the fenders. Just to the south of us a flock of egrets rose off a shallow lake in a huge white cloud of beating wings. "Pretty, ain't they?" Ira said. I nodded and watched the birds bank eastward toward the heart of the swamp to feed at some creek or shallow-water fishing ground that probably nobody but them knew about.

A few miles further on we turned off the oystershell road and onto the mucky prairie. At any other time of year the ground out here would be at least a foot underwater and way too soft for regular truck tires. You'd need a swamp buggy to get around. Only the tracts of high ground called hammocks stay above water during the rainy season. We were headed for the same place where we'd camped the year before, a big hardwood hammock with a clearing in it large enough for the trucks. We'd learned about it from an old boy named Weeks who knew the Big Cypress like his own backyard, and used to make his living poaching gator hides. There's the open prairie all around it, and a deep pinewoods about a hundred yards to the south and east, and a wide slough stretches north from it to connect with a creek next to a cluster of cypress heads way off in the distance. Great white-tail country.

But even in this driest time of year, our wheels spun in the muck and the trucks fishtailed as we closed in on the hammock through the high grass and the scrub palmettos. Mud flew off the tires until we reached firmer ground at the edge of the hammock, and then the trucks lurched up and into the clearing. And there we were, a fine long way from the world of jobs and bosses and wives and wanting to be someplace else.

This was the someplace else we were always wanting to be.

We were up and about before dawn, looking like ghosts in the chilly mist. We boiled water on a small propane stove and made instant coffee to wash down a breakfast of packaged pecan rolls. Charlie and Floyd put a smack of bourbon in their coffee but the rest of us said no thanks. How their stomachs can stand a prank like that at such an hour of the morning I don't know. We spoke in whispers as we put on our gear and loaded our rifles, metal sliding and snapping and clicking on metal. Everybody was a touch hungover, naturally, but feeling good, eager, grinning at each other the way we used to when we played football for Gulfside High and were suiting up for a game.

The eastern sky was purple now, and the dark tree lines were taking shape in the first grey light. I hobbled to the edge of the hammock where it sloped down to the muddy slough and I sat down at the base of a gumbo tree and made myself comfortable. As soon as the sun was up, my binoculars would give me a clear view of the open prairie and pinewoods beyond it—and all the way up the slough to the creek at the distant cypress heads.

The horizon was showing a bright streak of pink when everybody set off in different directions. Zeller and Ira went east. They preferred still-hunting, so they'd each find themselves a camouflaged spot somewhere in the pines and just sit there waiting for a deer to come walking by. Floyd and Charlie didn't have that kind of patience. They'd stay on the move and try to jump a deer out of hiding. Charlie went into the south pineland and Floyd headed up the slough toward the cypress heads.

There's nothing quiet about a swamp, not even in broad daylight. The bugs never let up their buzzing and chirping, and there's birdcalls and frogs ringing and always something rustling around in the brush or splooshing in the water. When you're with somebody, you're not even aware of the other noise around you, but when you're sitting out there all by yourself you realize what a commotion it really is.

Every now and then a jetliner rumbled way up high as it headed into or out of Miami. Once in a while I heard gunfire. There were other hunters in the area, and every time I heard a shot I wondered if it was one of us banging at a deer.

By late afternoon I was bored silly and feeling sorry for myself for being stuck in camp with a bad foot. I was eating a Spam sandwich and looking off to the north when something came out of the cypress trees. I thought it might be a deer and my heart took a hop as I tossed away the sandwich and grabbed up the field glasses to have a better look.

It was only Floyd. He had his rifle on its sling over his shoulder and was starting to go around a flag pond to head back this way. Just then he glanced over to his right and stopped in his tracks. I panned over about twenty yards in the direction he was looking. And there, across the little pond and right where the creek curved around the far end of the cypress head, was the biggest whitetail buck I've ever seen.

It was standing a good fifteen feet out from the trees and looking my way. I almost yanked the binoculars away from my eyes, feeling for a crazy second like it could see me as clearly as I was seeing him—which of course it couldn't, not from that far off. Then it moseyed up to the edge of the creek as casual as you please and dipped its head for a drink. It looked to be at least a twelve-pointer, but it was hard to say for sure at that distance.

I panned back to Floyd. He was standing like a statue. I knew he was thinking that if he made the slightest motion the buck would bolt. But since the deer wasn't going to stand there till it died of old age, Floyd had to make his move. He slowly slid his hand up his shirt to his shoulder and hooked his thumb under the rifle sling. I swung the glasses back to the deer and saw that it was still drinking. If I hadn't been absolutely sure it was beyond range of my little carbine I would have taken a shot at it myself, even from this distance. I would've caught hell from Floyd, naturally, since he was closer and had the cleaner shot, but so what?

Now Floyd was hoisting the rifle off his shoulder by the sling and *slowly* bringing it around in front of him. You could see that he was downwind of the buck—the grass was leaning toward him in the slight breeze—but even though the deer hadn't caught his scent it was purely amazing it hadn't seen him standing there, just sixty, seventy feet away. I was swinging the binoculars from one to the other like I was at a tennis match.

In slow motion, Floyd brought the rifle up to port arms and then just stood there. I couldn't understand why he was taking so long to aim and shoot. Finally it dawned on me that for safety's sake he didn't have a bullet in the chamber. He'd have to work the lever to load a round—and when he did that, the deer would hear the lever's action and scoot away into the trees before he could get off a shot. Just the same, there wasn't anything else for him to do but to do it, so he slowly pushed open the lever.

The buck dipped its head for another drink. Floyd closed the lever and the round was loaded. I couldn't believe the buck didn't hear the lever working. Could the animal be so sorrowfully afflicted that it was both nearsighted and hard of hearing? Now Floyd had the Winchester to his shoulder and was taking aim. So long, buck, I thought.

A wisp of pale smoke puffed from the muzzle a fraction of a second before I heard the crack of the shot. The buck jerked its head up and hopped a step to the side. Sometimes a shot is so absolutely perfect that the animal is dead on its feet before its legs give out from under it, and that's what I thought happened this time.

But the buck was still standing there and looking over at Floyd, and I finally realized it hadn't even been hit. It seemed impossible for Floyd to have missed that shot: a full side-view and practically point-blank. But just as unbelievable was the deer not running away after hearing that bang from the .30-.30 and catching sight of Floyd. All it did was stand there and look at him.

Floyd must've been as stunned as I was that he'd missed, but he recovered pretty fast. He worked the lever again and aimed ... and *pow*.

Nothing. The buck twitched its ears and seemed to sniff at the air but otherwise didn't make a move.

Floyd took a step back and held the rifle out in front of him in both hands like it was some strange thing he'd never seen before. He double-jacked a round in and out of the chamber and picked up the cartridge and gave it a close inspection. I figured he was checking to see if somebody had played a trick on him and put blanks in the magazine when he wasn't looking. That would've been a good trick, all right, if somebody had thought of it, especially Charlie, who was prone to that sort of thing. Floyd saw they weren't blanks, though, and he tossed the round aside. He looked at the deer still standing there and took a long careful aim at it once more.

Pow! The buck's ears twirled and its tail flapped a couple of times, but it stayed right where it was. Floyd put a hand to his face. Then he looked at the deer again, worked the lever, took a couple of steps closer to the edge of the pond, and drew another bead.

Pow! The buck looked around like it was maybe wondering what Floyd was shooting at. I tell you, I didn't believe what I was seeing. I still don't believe it.

Floyd fired again and missed again. The deer stood in place and did a sort of little dance and twitched its ears. Floyd lowered the gun and wiped at his eyes. I saw his shoulders give a heave. Lots of people might make fun of a grown man crying right out in the open like that, but not me. I saw what he was going through, saw it with my own eyes. It was something to cry about.

Just the same, he had one round left in the magazine and he had to fire it, no matter how much he'd already been humiliated. He must've known he was going to miss again; I knew he was going to miss again. It wouldn't have made one bit of sense if he did anything *but* miss again. I felt sorrier for Floyd than I know how to say.

He wiped at his eyes again, then at his nose, then walked up to the edge of the pond, which put him about five yards closer to the buck. Then took aim. Then *pow*.

The deer stood there and shook its head, I swear it did. Shook that big rack of antlers like it might have been thinking the world was full of fools. Then it turned and started for the trees, but moving in no hurry at all.

That's when Floyd started to howl. He sounded like a thin, faraway siren. He howled and turned in a tight circle, then gripped the rifle by the end of the barrel like a softball bat and started running after the deer, splashing through the knee-high water in the flag pond and hollering to high heaven. The buck glanced back at him and started stepping a little higher toward the trees, but it still didn't bolt. Floyd staggered out of the pond and flung the rifle whirling with both hands and missed the buck by a good ten feet. He dropped to his knees and grabbed up rocks and sticks, clods of muck, anything, and threw all that too, still hollering.

At the edge of the cypress head the buck stopped and gave another look back at him, then flapped its white tail a couple of quick times and jumped into the trees and was gone.

Ira told me later that when he heard Floyd's first shot so nearby he didn't know it was Floyd, but he wanted to see if somebody had put down a deer, so he doubled back to the slough to have a look. As he made his way through the trees, he heard the other shots one after the other and he knew something wasn't right. He came out of the pines about midway between the camp and the cypress head just in time to see Floyd miss the buck with his last shot. And he witnessed the awful things that followed: Floyd chasing after the deer and throwing his rifle at it, throwing rocks and sticks, and yelling like a lunatic the whole time. The spectacle was so unreal Ira couldn't think of what to do but hustle straight back to camp.

As we watched Floyd trudging his slow way back along the slough with his rifle across his shoulders, I told Ira the whole horrifying story of how he had missed the buck six times altogether.

"Lordy, Jake," he said, staring big eyed out at Floyd coming toward us, "you don't reckon he's lost his mind, do you?"

Ira has always tended to get somewhat unnerved by the unnatural or hard-to-explain. That's a bad way to be in a world that seems stranger and crazier every day. Not that he can't take care of himself. He's got a punch like a mulekick. Just last month he put his fist through the windshield of Lamar Boyd's Dakota because Lamar bet him ten dollars he couldn't do it. He's not afraid of any man alive, but the strangeness of the world can sometimes spook him bad. About six months ago he'd even tried being born-again to find some way to deal with the weirdness of life, but he got kicked out of the congregation when he got drunk at a church picnic and grabbed the preacher's wife's ass. That's also one of the latest reasons his wife Kay Marie is living at her sister's and filing for divorce, even though Ira keeps begging her to forgive him and come home.

"Listen, Jake," he said, "a man can't miss a deer that many times from that close. It ain't natural. And what kinda deer just stands there—one that ain't jacklit, I mean—just stands there and lets a man shoot at it over and over? What kinda deer shakes its head at a man? You got to admit, it ain't natural."

He was right, it wasn't natural, but I didn't see what there was to be done about it, so I just shrugged and lit up a cigarette and watched Floyd make his way back to camp. He came up out of the slough all muddy and dragging the rifle by the barrel. He looked pale and a touch wall-eyed, like a man who's taken a hard punch to the head and hasn't quite shaken it off yet. Ira went to the truck and came back stripping the seal off a bottle of Jim Beam bourbon. He took a big bubbling drink and then passed the bottle to Floyd. A couple of deep swallows put some color back in his face and a little focus in his eyes. We passed the bottle around for a minute and then Floyd finally broke the silence: "You all *see* it?"

Ira and I took a quick look at each other and then nodded. "Yeah," Ira said, "I ... we ... Jake and me ... yeah."

Floyd gave a huge snort of disgust and took another long drink, and gave the bottle back to Ira. He went to sit under a pine and set the carbine across his lap and laced his hands together on top of his head the way he always does when he's trying hard to figure something that's got him confused.

A couple of minutes later here came Zeller wanting to know what all the shooting was about. He looked at Ira and then at me and then at Floyd sitting under the tree. "Hey, what's going on?" he said.

Ira went up close to him and told him the story in a half-whisper. As he listened, Zeller glanced over at Floyd and pretty soon started grinning. Floyd was staring off across the slough and not paying them any attention.

Suddenly Zeller laughed and said, "Oh, *bull*shit! You don't think I believe that." Then he saw the look Floyd was giving him and he shut up.

Just then we heard a rifleshot from the pinewoods to the south, over where Charlie had gone. We listened hard, waiting to hear if more shots would follow, but none did.

"If that's Charlie …," Floyd said in a voice so low it was almost scary. "If he got him a deer with one damn shot…" His mouth went tight and he looked up at the sky like God alone knew what thing might happen.

What Charlie got with that one shot was a humongous diamondback rattler. He came strutting into camp with a wide grin and the thing draped over his shoulder. Except for Floyd, who was too busy feeling sorry for himself, we all gathered around Charlie for a better look. He pulled it off his neck and let it slide to the ground. It was a good five feet long and as big around as a beer bottle, and had a raw wound about three inches below the head.

"I didn't want to damage the head or the best part of the skin," Charlie said. "I'm gonna use that head for a gearshift knob on my truck. And that hide's going up on the living-room wall, and Hallie Anne best not give me any grief about it." He was trying to be cool about the whole thing but it was hard for him to contain his excitement. I couldn't blame him. It was some snake.

"You shoulda *seen* the way it moved," Charlie said. "Quick as a damn whip. I kept trying to get up close for a clean shot under the head, and it kept striking at me from ten feet away, I ain't lying! It was like we was doing some kind of dance. But I finally got the shot."

It had a head on it the size of my fist and a set of rattles big as an ear of corn. Charlie took out his buck knife and said, "Rattler steak for supper, boys!" He cut off the rattles and shook them at us with a grin. Even detached from a dead snake it's a sound to raise the hair on your neck. He wrapped the rattles in a bandana and stuck them in his pocket, then he cut off the head all nice and neat and held it up for us to admire.

That's when he noticed Floyd sitting by himself and staring off at nothing. "Hey," Charlie said. "What's with you?" Just as Floyd turned to look at him Charlie said, "Think fast!" and with a quick underhand move he threw the snake head at him.

Floyd dodged the head with a sideways roll as smooth as if he'd practiced it all his life, and came up on one knee with the Winchester at his hip and pointed at Charlie. John Wayne couldn't have done it better. Charlie stood there with his mouth open, staring down the barrel of Floyd's carbine.

For a second or two nobody moved. Then Floyd looked at the rifle in his hands and said, "Hell, I'd probably miss by five feet," and he tossed the gun aside.

"You crazy sumbitch!" Charlie hollered. "Point a gun at *me*!" He started for Floyd, but Ira grabbed onto his arm and said, "Wait a minute, man, listen!" But Charlie was too hacked off to do anything but cuss a blue streak and try to shake Ira off and get to Floyd—who quick got up and ran into the trees.

Now Zeller grabbed Charlie by the other arm, and I gimped up from behind and got him in a headlock, and all of us were saying for him to be cool and take it easy and so on, but Charlie just snarled like a pit bull and took us all down in a struggling heap, yelling that he would by God kick all our asses.

We wrestled around like that for the next few minutes, everybody cussing and grunting and getting all red in the face, all of us trying to tell Charlie that Floyd didn't mean it, and the rifle wasn't loaded anyway, and if he'd only listen for a minute, dammit, he'd understand why Floyd had been so touchy.

It took a while, but Charlie finally heard what we were saying, as we held him down in a sweaty tangle of arms and legs, with our noses bloody and our faces scratched up and our shirttails up around our chests and all of us really sucking for breath now.

"Are you ... telling me," Charlie said, huffing hard, "he had ... *six* shots ... at a deer? Same deer?"

"And missed ... ever one," Zeller said.

"From hardly ... no farther ... than me to you," Ira said.

"It ain't nothing ... but the truth," I said. "I saw ... the whole thing ... start to finish."

Charlie quit his struggling altogether then and started laughing. Not like Zeller, who'd laughed because he couldn't believe it. Charlie laughed because he did.

We pondered the thing plenty while we sat around the fire drinking whiskey from our canteen cups. Thick strips of peppered rattlesnake roasted on sticks propped against the firestones. The sun was below the treeline now, and the western sky was a long bright blaze of orange. A chill was rising out of the sloughs. The aroma of sizzling snake meat mingled with the ripe evening smells of the swamp. Owls hooted in the high pines.

We took turns inspecting the Winchester from every which way, and came up with all kinds of possible explanations for what happened. The sights were off. The rifling in the barrel wasn't true. The barrel was improperly mounted on the stock. The cartridges were poorly packed. And so on and so forth. But I could tell that nobody else, including Floyd, believed any of those excuses any more than I did. The plain and simple truth was that the rifle and bullets looked fine.

Finally Charlie said what I'd been thinking, but didn't have the heart to tell Floyd to his face, at least not while he was feeling so bad. The others must've been thinking it too. "Had to've been buck fever," Charlie said. "It ain't no other explanation for it."

Floyd looked at Charlie like he'd accused him of wearing women's underpants. Buck fever's when a man spots a deer but gets too excited to shoot straight. It's something that's not supposed to happen to an experienced hunter, but sometimes it does. It's an accusation that'll rile any man, and Floyd was already pretty riled as it was. And the bourbon he'd been drinking hadn't done a thing to improve his mood.

He gave Charlie a hard look and said, "Hey, mullethead, I ain't never had buck fever in my whole entire life."

"Hell, boy, it ain't nothing to be shamed of," Charlie said with a big smile. "Can happen to any man—even if it ain't never happened to me."

"Could be it was buck fever," Ira said. "But that don't

explain why that buck didn't run off when Floyd shot at him. You all got to admit, it just ain't natural for a deer to stand there while a man shoots at him over and over."

"After Floyd missed him from practically point-blank, he didn't see no *need* to run off," Charlie said. He gave Floyd another grin and Floyd gave him the finger.

"And what about the way he shook his head?" Ira said. "He stood right there and shook his head. I saw him do it and Jake did too. Now that ain't natural neither."

"He was probably trying to shake the ringing out of his head," Zeller said. "All that shooting, right in his ear practically, he's likely walking around deaf as a fence post this minute."

"It wasn't no damn buck fever," Floyd said, pouring himself another drink. "You ever hear of anybody with buck fever for six straight shots? No way."

"Six *straight* shots?" Zeller said, smiling around his tin cup. "Any of them shots been straight, we'd be fixing to eat venison instead of snake for supper."

Everybody thought that was funny but Floyd. Charlie had been fooling with the rattler head all the while, and now he held it out in front of him and said to it, "You hear that, old son? These boys ruther eat deer meat than you. Enough to make you feel low, ain't it?" He tilted the snake head down and shook it from side to side, like it was feeling shame.

"Maybe it was a ghost buck," I said with a big grin. Floyd gave me a look like those I get from Brenda a half-dozen times a day. She's always accusing me of making jokes about things I don't understand. One time I said if that was true I'd do nothing but make jokes about *her* all day long. And the fight was on.

"If it was a ghost buck, that would sure enough explain why Floyd couldn't kill it," Ira said. He looked so serious I had to laugh.

"Lookey here, boys," Charlie said, holding the rattler head up beside his own. He'd quit using a cup and was drinking straight from the bottle. "Me and my friend here think you ought to quit all this talk of ghosty deer and such. The man had buck fever and that's all there is to it." He worked his hand up and down so that the snake head seemed to be nodding in agreement. "Ain't a thing in the world for the man to be ashamed of," he gave Floyd another big grin, "even if he did have the fever for six shots in a row, which for sure got to be a world's record. Hell, could happen to any man—especially any man who's real old and blind."

"Buck fever, my ass," Floyd said. He glared at the Winchester. "It's that rifle. She did something to it."

"Who did?" Ira said.

"That bitch I'm married to, who you think? She had something done to it is why I couldn't hit nothing. Acting all sweet and like she wants to make up, then gives me a gun can't hit a deer from here to there. She's probably laughing right this minute thinking about me trying to shoot something with it."

Such an idea hadn't crossed my mind—or anybody else's, to judge from the momentary silence that followed.

Then Ira said, "There's that old gypsy fortuneteller on the old highway in Bonita. You think Carol might've took your gun to her and had a curse put on it?"

Charlie whooped at that and I laughed in the middle of taking a drink, and the whiskey came up through my nose and burned the hell out of my sinuses. Zeller said, "Oh, for crissake," and looked at Ira like he was the most pathetic thing he'd ever seen.

"All I know is I'm gonna put a curse on *her*," Floyd said. "I'm gonna put a curse on her *ass*."

"Why don't you let my buddy here give her a little bite on the ass for you?" Charlie said. "Look here at the teeth on this old boy." He pulled back the skin around the snake's mouth to reveal its fangs. They were long and curved and fine pointed and gleamed in the firelight.

"He sure enough tried to stick me with these," Charlie said. "But see here how a rattler got to open his mouth real wide to use them?"

Holding the snake head with its mouth wide and fangs bared, he demonstrated the rattler's striking action. "Like that, see? Say you were reaching for something near its nest and you didn't hear them rattles till your hand was down close to it. He'd do just like this."

He put his free hand out in front of him and flicked the rattler head at it—and one of the fangs snagged his middle finger just behind the middle knuckle.

He stared at the snake head hooked to his hand and said softly, "Son of a bitch."

The rest of us all busted out laughing. Charlie gently extracted the fang and examined his finger. We all leaned forward for a better look. It was a small dark puncture with no blood.

"Son of a *bitch*!" He looked at the snake head like it had just insulted his momma. Then he wound up and threw it hard against a tree trunk barely four feet away, and the head ricocheted like a rock and missed Zeller's head by a whisker.

"Hey, you stupid buttface!" Zeller hollered.

"It bit me! The thing *bit* me!"

"That's no reason to hit somebody in the head with the damn thing!"

"I'm *poisoned*, dammit!"

"I hope to hell you are," Zeller said. "You near got me in the face with it."

"I don't believe a man can *be* poisoned by no dead snake," Ira said.

"Really?" Charlie said. "Is that true, Ira? You telling me true?" He swung around to me. "That true, Jake, what he said?" I had nearly three years of college and they never quit making fun of me for it, but any time they need the facts about something to settle a bet I'm the man they turn to.

I said I'd never heard of anybody dying from the bite of a dead snake. "Then again," I said, "I never heard of anybody getting *bit* by a dead snake either."

"It ain't gonna do you harm, boy," Ira told Charlie. "Not a bite from just the *head*. If it was a whole snake, there might be some question about it, but not just the head."

"That's about the dumbest thing I ever heard," Zeller said. "Where you think the poison's at, in his tail?"

"Hey, peckerwood," Ira said, "when Charlie cut the head off, didn't the blood drain out of it? Damn sure did. Well, why wouldn't the poison drain out too? Can't answer me *that*, can you?"

"I swear, you are so ignorant you don't even know how damn ignorant you are," Zeller said.

"Sticks and stones," Ira said and made a prissy face at him.

"All I know," I said, "is we *could* stand around talking about it for the rest of the night, or we might tend to that bite, just in case."

We sat Charlie in front of a truck headlight so we could see what we were doing. Even though Floyd's buck knife was already sharp enough to split hairs, he gave the blade a few more licks on a sharpening stone. Then Zeller poured whiskey all along the edge of the knife and over the puncture wound in Charlie's finger. Then we passed the bottle all around and took another little drink to ready ourselves.

"You ain't got to cut real deep, you know," Charlie told Floyd. "Only takes two little bitty cuts is all." He turned his face away and grit his teeth as Floyd made a small incision on either side of the puncture.

"There—all done," Floyd said.

"You're supposed to suck the poison out of them cuts," Charlie said, holding his finger out to Floyd.

Floyd feinted at the finger with the knife like he was gonna cut it off, and Charlie snatched his hand back and laughed and set to cleaning out the wound himself by repeatedly sucking on it and spitting a red streak.

"This reminds me of the one about the two old boys who were out hunting, and one got bit on the ass by a rattler," Zeller said. "Didn't neither one of them know any first aid, but they had a mobile phone in the truck, and the one old boy tells the one who's bit to just lay still, and he'll go call a doctor and find out what to do. So he goes back to the truck and calls up, and the doc tells him he's got to make a couple of cuts on the snake bite and suck out the poison. So the old boy goes back to where his friend's still laying, and his friend asks him what the doctor said. And the old boy tells him, 'He says you're gonna die.'"

We'd all heard that one before, but now it seemed extra funny to everybody but Charlie. He glared around at us as Zeller poured a little more whiskey on his finger, and Ira put a Band-Aid on it. Charlie worked his hand into a fist a few times and said the finger hurt.

"Well hell, it's supposed to hurt *some*," Ira said. "You had a snake tooth in it."

We settled back around the fire to eat our supper of burned snake meat and opened up another bottle of bourbon. We made fun of Charlie for a while, then listened to Floyd tell how he was going to kick Carol's ass black-and-blue for giving him that tricked-up rifle. By the time I crawled into my sleeping bag, the only one still sitting by the fire was Charlie. He was still taking drinks from the bottle and holding his bad hand in his lap like it was a hurt pet.

I woke up shivering in the middle of the night. My tongue

tasted like something dead in the road a week and my head
was pounding bad. The campfire was down to a bed of bright
orange coals. I heard somebody hissing, "Floyd! Floyd, wake
up! Floyd!" It was Charlie. In the glow of the coal fire I saw
him squatting beside Floyd and shaking him by the shoulder.
"Floyd! Listen to me!" You could hear how drunk he was.

Floyd stirred and growled and tried to shake off Charlie's
hand. Then he lifted his head and said, "Huh? What?"

"You my friend, ain't you, Floyd?"

"Huh?" Floyd said. He propped himself up on an elbow.
"*What?* Charlie." He was still fairly drunk himself.

"Floyd, you my friend, ain't you?" Charlie said. "You gotta
help me, Floyd. Lookit." He held his hand up against the low
light of the fire so Floyd could see it. I could see it clear
enough to see that the middle finger was swollen as big as a
hot dog.

"Damn," Floyd said and sat up.

"You gotta cut it off, Floyd," Charlie said. "It's the only
thing to do. It's fulla poison and if you don't cut it off I'm
gonna die. *Help* me, Floyd."

He took out his hunting knife, a huge thing with a blade
nearly a foot long, and put it in Floyd's hand. "Here," he said.
"I sharpened it up real good already." He reached behind him
and pulled over the small flat-topped chunk of wood he'd
used for cutting the snake meat, and he spread his hand flat on
it, the middle finger huge. "Come *on*, Floyd! It's no time to
lose, man."

And damn if Floyd didn't get up on his knees and hold
Charlie's bad hand in place on the cutting board and set the
edge of the knife blade right at the finger's top joint.

I was scrambling toward them on hands and knees and
yelling and Floyd was just starting to press down on the knife
when Ira went by me in a low rush that drew up sparks from
the fire, and he tackled Floyd so hard the breath blasted out of

both of them as they tumbled away from Charlie, and the knife went sailing off into the dark.

We got Charlie to the emergency room just before dawn. Zeller and I rode with him in the open bed of his truck while Floyd drove. Ira followed us in his own truck, which was carrying all our gear. As we broke camp Floyd sobered up enough to realize what he'd almost done and he cussed Charlie up and down for a dumb peckerwood, but we kept giving Charlie whiskey to ease the pain of his finger, and he was too drunk to pay Floyd any mind. By the time we got to the hospital, he was even drunker than when he'd begged Floyd to cut off his finger.

Ira and Zeller each got Charlie by an arm and hustled him into the bright lights of the emergency admitting room. Zeller had Charlie's wallet so he could provide the information for the admission forms. Charlie kept trying to break loose of them. He was so drunk he thought they were entering a movie-theater lobby. "What the hell we doing at the show?" he hollered. "I wanna go *hunting*, dammit!"

Because of my bad foot, I waited in the cab of Ira's truck, and because Floyd didn't want to even look at Charlie, he waited out there with me. Twenty minutes later here came Ira and Zeller in a big hurry. A doctor had told them Charlie would have to stay in the hospital for at least one night, and a nurse had telephoned Hallie Anne, who said she'd be right over. We figured we'd best be on our way before she got there.

Zeller and Floyd followed me and Ira down the road to a 7-11 store for coffee-to-go as the sun came flaring up over the trees. Then we went to Charlie's house. When we turned onto his street we slowed down till we saw for sure that Hallie Anne's Camaro was already gone. Then Floyd gunned the Jimmy up into the driveway and cut the engine, and him and

Zeller came running back to Ira's truck and jumped in, and off we went.

Zeller's house was closest from Charlie's, so we dropped him off first. He got his gear out of the back and said so long, and as he started lugging his stuff to the carport his wife Suzanne came hurrying out the front door to give him a hand. She's got blond down to her ass and freckles across her nose, and the greatest smile in the world. She waved to us as we drove off, and I wished we'd stayed a while and gone in the house and let her smile at us some more, and fix us coffee and something to eat like she always does when Zeller brings any of us to his house. She always makes you feel like she's really glad to see you, because you're a friend of Zeller's and that's good enough for her. Zeller hardly ever talks about her. Anytime the rest of us complain about our wives he looks almost embarrassed, like the only guy in good health when everybody around him is sick with the same thing.

Floyd's was the next stop. He lives in a nice double-wide on ten acres his daddy gave him for his twenty-first birthday. The property's got a creek and sits way out in the boonies between the airport road and the interstate. Not a neighbor for miles around, which is one of the best things about it.

On the way there, Floyd started getting worked up about the rifle all over again, muttering low and cussing Carol for whatever she'd done to it so it couldn't shoot straight. By the time we turned in at his front gate and onto the dirt drive leading to his house, he was even hotter about it than he'd been the day before. Ira and I couldn't help laughing, which only made him hotter because he didn't think it was one bit funny.

The driveway curves around a thick windbreak of Australian pines before the house comes into view. And there Carol was, working in shorts and T-shirt in her flower garden alongside the house. A little further back, Floyd's Bronco and his trailered jon boat were parked in the shade of a big live oak. She saw us coming and sat back on her heels and tugged down the bill of her blue KC Royals cap.

"Look at her," Floyd said. "Little Miss Innocent."

"Probably wondering what we're doing back so soon," I said.

"She oughta be wondering how she's gonna put her ass back together when I'm done kicking it," Floyd said.

Before the truck came to a full stop, Floyd was out of the cab and yanking the sheath off the rifle and stomping over toward Carol, yelling, "Real funny, girl! Real damn funny! You cost me the biggest buck in the world because of this gun!"

She looked halfway between confused and wanting to get mad right back at him. "What? What are you hollering about? You saying the gun doesn't work right?"

"Oh, man, listen to you. 'Don't it *work* right?' As if you didn't know."

"Floyd, I don't know *what* you're—"

"Liar—liar!" He whipped the rifle around by the barrel and let it fly. It whirled through the air and tore into the middle of her garden like a propeller blade, and sent up a spray of dirt and ripped flowers. Carol jumped up with a look like he'd just thrown a baby into an alligator pit.

"Take these, too!" he yelled, digging cartridges out of his jacket pockets and flinging them at her. "They're worth squat in that damn gun!"

She held her hands in front of her in that funny way women do to try and protect themselves, but a couple of the bullets hit her in the legs and she yipped. "Stop it!" she said. "Stop it, Floyd!"

But Floyd kept right on tossing bullets at her, which we all realized at about the same time was a really dumb thing to do—because Carol all of a sudden said, "Oh, God *damn* it!" and snatched up some of the shells and grabbed up the rifle, and quick shoved a few rounds in the magazine and jacked one into the chamber.

Ira and I bumped heads so hard I saw stars as we ducked down below the dashboard. The shot was the loudest I ever heard in my life. *Pow!*

"Oh, Lord *Jesus*," Ira said.

Then, *Pow!* and we flinched again. And *Pow!* again.

Then there wasn't a sound except for our ragged breathing.

"Sweet baby Jesus," Ira whispered, all big-eyed. "Is she gonna kill us too, you think?"

I eased up real slow for a look over the dash and saw Carol resting the rifle barrel on her shoulder. It wouldn't have surprised me a bit to see her standing with one foot up on Floyd's dead body. But Floyd was peeking up from behind Ira's front fender where he'd taken cover. He was staring off toward his Bronco and looking like he'd just gotten some real bad news. I followed his gaze over to the vehicle, and saw that the windshield had a starburst hole, the spotlight by the driver's door was shattered and hanging loose on its joint, and the left front tire was flat as can be.

Ira arched up and took a careful peek and said, "Boy, howdy."

"Seems to be working just fine *now*, doesn't it?" Carol called out, real sarcastic. She threw the rifle down and marched off to the front door and turned around and hollered, "Floyd, you *dickhead*! *All* you!" Then she went in and slammed the door as loud as another rifle shot.

Floyd looked at us through the windshield but I couldn't read a thing in his face. He started walking toward the Bronco, then veered toward the rifle, then hesitated and changed course again and headed for the house. He stopped a few feet from the front door and stood staring at it for a moment, and then laced his hands on top of his head, squashing the crown of his camouflaged cap. He stayed that way for at least a full minute, looking sort of like a prisoner of war waiting for an order. Then he dropped his hands and went inside.

Now Floyd's saying he's done with hunting forever and Charlie's still not talking to anybody. But it's been more than a week now, and me and Ira and Zeller figure they'll both get over it pretty soon. Charlie'll finally have to admit there's nobody to blame but himself for nearly getting his finger cut off. And even though Floyd says he's mad at Charlie for talking him into nearly cutting it off and making them the butt of a lot of jokes at The Dog House, the real reason he's mad is that he knows Charlie was right about the buck fever. I mean, it *had* to have been buck fever. I don't know why that buck didn't spook and run—Ira's right, it wasn't natural—but buck fever's the only logical explanation for Floyd missing that deer from that close, even for missing six times. We all know it and Floyd knows it too.

Anyway, there's another reason he's sure to quit this foolishness about not hunting anymore. Some of the old boys at The Dog House are saying that Carol's got him pretty well whipped since she shot up his vehicle. They're saying *she's* the one decided Floyd wasn't ever going hunting again. Of course, me and Ira and Zeller don't believe that for a minute. Not a man among us thinks Floyd's *that* bad off. We figure he'll pretty soon feel obliged to put the lie to that mean talk. That's why there's a good chance we'll all be heading back into the Big Cypress before the end of the season, even if we have to do it during the Christmas holidays. The wives will raise hell about it, naturally, but there's not a thing in the world new about that.

George Manner

Here I am, dominating space.

George Manner, born in Louisiana, spent the last eighteen years in Houston before moving recently to Santa Fe, New Mexico, where he teaches at Santa Fe Community College. In 1984 he won the PEN Southwest Discovery Prize for Poetry. He has published in, among others, the *Southern Review, Shenandoah, Gulf Coast,* and, in the UK, the *Realto,* as well as in two anthologies, *The Montana Poets Anthology* ('79) and *A Trout in the Milk.*

GEORGE MANNER
The Gravestone Carver Speaks

I must be getting old: it's almost as quiet outside
as inside me now. All these years of marble dust rinsed
from my hair, neck, all the old familiar trails it took down
my body—Jude above, tipping her dim grey pail.
All these years chipping away
inscriptions that never could say....
And all the red-eyed people speaking softly, so as not
to awaken the sleeping baby they sensed to be in the back
far corner of my shop. It was never there.
Oh we thought about it some, back when passion mainly
ordered our lives. Sometimes, from the chalk Sunday mornings
are made of, Jude would murmur me awake, murmur
about a son. I'm quieter now, which is fine. I plan
what I'll eat, drink fruit juice only before noon, close
the day down with milk and books. I find myself reading
more and more writers who, themselves, grew old,
quieter, as shouting hurts my ears and the energy and
gesture seem a waste.
My hands are still good, my arms strong. I remember,
early on, the challenges: the B, J, Q, R, S and U;
the exact, deep period—how it should stand for someone
having been; spacing dilemmas that had more to do with me
than with the deceased; weather. And, much later,
I remember sensing that my own time was coming:

the foolish battle I had with myself, should I or should I
not write, then gouge, my own stone so as to lift
that weight from the town. But I recall other things as well:
how the rock would heat up in summer, the sun distributed
inside; the time, overnight!, three cicadas left their shells
on my shop door, and how those husks weathered two major storms,
then a third; how Jude would weave between
the stood samples with my sandwich and apple and iced
water or tea, the gold hair on her neck darkening
against her moist skin. I remember working Jude's stone:
never have I been so far from myself, never have I heard so well
what was going on outside me—the birds, children
just off from school, the grass's imagined cry of pain
as I shifted my weight. The question of working my own
stone is easy now. I will. But what to say?, for there is
no one I have to speak to, no heir. Perhaps
instead of language, or in spite of it, I will

suffer my stone to uphold pictures
from my childhood *Book of Facts*.
Upper left,
our modern world's largest bird, the Peruvian condor;
upper right,
a quarter moon to fly to;
wheat in wind across the middle;
below my name and dates a descending series of fish—
the first a trout,
the second a sturgeon,
the third one's prehistoric and nosing off into an area
I have chiselled
to encourage the growth of algae.

April Poetry Open
1st-, 2nd-, and 3rd-Place Winners

First-place winner: GEORGE MANNER
"The Gravestone Carver Speaks"
George Manner receives $500 for his first-place poem, which begins on page 43, preceded by his profile on page 42.

Second-place winner: ARIANA-SOPHIA KARTSONIS
"Vanishing Armenia"
Ariana-Sophia Kartsonis's work has appeared or is forthcoming in Amaranth, Hayden's Ferry Review, Painted Bride Quarterly, Princeton Arts Review, and the Patterson Literary Review.
"Vanishing Armenia" is dedicated and indebted to Daniel Varoujan and Diana Der Hovanessian.

Third-place winner: SIMONE MUENCH
"Eating Olives in the House of Heartbroken Women"
Simone Muench is the associate editor for ACM (Another Chicago Magazine). Her work has appeared in Crab Orchard Review, Many Mountains Moving, Southern Poetry Review, Bloomsbury Review, Calyx, Luna, and others. She comes from Shreveport, Louisiana, but received her BA and MA from the University of Colorado. Her manuscript "Love's Apostrophes" won the 1998 Sheila-Na-Gig Chapbook Contest. She recently was selected to receive an Illinois Arts Council Award for a poem published in Fish Stories.

We invite you to our website (www.glimmertrain.com) to see a listing of the top twenty-five winners and finalists. We thank all entrants for sending in their work.

Margo Rabb

*Me at the easel. I've been told I preferred
eating the paints to painting with them.*

Margo Rabb was born and raised in Queens, New York. She lives in Tucson, Arizona, where she received an MFA from the University of Arizona. Recently she received first prize in the *Atlantic Monthly* student-writing contest. She has had stories in *Seventeen, American Fiction, Witness, Chicago Review*, and the *Atlantic Monthly*, and has broadcast on National Public Radio. "How to Find Love" is from a linked collection of stories she is writing about the narrator and her family during the year after her mother died.

MARGO RABB
How to Find Love

ow do you fall in love?
This was what I awoke wondering the morning I turned
sixteen. It was August, during one of New York's record heat
waves; even my bedroom windows seemed to sweat. When I
opened my eyes all I could think was that it wouldn't be so
bad to wake up sweating, if, as in movies and romance
novels and dramas on TV, you awoke beside somebody else.

But there wasn't anyone else. In our quiet, empty house,
my single bed was filled only with pancake-flat, fur-mangled
stuffed animals, steamrolled from years of being slept on. For
ages my father had been trying to get me to throw them
out; he'd only given up recently, after my mother's death in
January, when I stood before my bears, rabbits, gorillas,
kangaroos, and, with all the passion of Scarlett O'Hara,
vowed in a fierce, husky voice, "*Never.*"

But now all I could think was, I was a sixteen-year-old
girl still sleeping with gorillas. Not like *Sixteen Candles*, or
any of those coming-of-age movies; there were no boyfriends, no hopes of boyfriends waiting outside my door.
Just my father, one room away, snoring on his side of my
parents' double bed.

Birthdays had been a big deal when my mother was alive:

Glimmer Train Stories, Issue 33, Winter 2000
©1999 Margo Rabb

parties with tons of kids pinning the tail on the donkey, batting piñatas, gorging on Duncan Hines SuperMoist cake with Fudge Frosting. We didn't have a lot of money but she always bought some surprise—a three-tiered set of Ultima II makeup, silver-plated hair clips—despite the groans of my father that we were killing him with the bills.

This year I knew what my father had gotten me—he'd left it in a bag in the hall closet—Teen Lady shampoo, body wash, and scented powder from the supermarket. He must've asked the store clerk, "What do you get for a *girl?*" and been told this. I often wished there was some guidebook I could give him, *How to Raise a Daughter* or something; he seemed near cardiac arrest when I asked for money for tampons, had no comprehension of the magic word "shopping," and thought re-upholstering the couch made for a fun Saturday night. In fact, the couch was now his whole existence; he'd retired on my mother's life-insurance money, and spent each day there reading the complete *New York Times*.

Every afternoon when I came home from school he'd narrate his day: "This morning I had myself a bagel with the no-fat cream cheese; lunch, a Wendy's grilled chicken. In Topeka they had a scandal with the honey-mustard sauce; people got sick I read on page six of the Living Section. I saved the article for you—" And I'd gaze longingly at the television, as if I could jump into a family on the set.

Aside from the Wendy's cashiers, I was often the only person he talked to during the day. "Why don't you bring your friends over, I'll bake a chicken?" he'd ask me. Or, "Invite Sarah, we'll play Scrabble," "Isabel can help us fix the bird feeder," or, "I bet Rebecca would like this Sherlock Holmes movie too." It didn't matter that I hadn't seen Sarah, Isabel, or Rebecca since sixth grade, or that if I asked them over now, they'd surely run off. Our house had become Spooky House, one of those run-down, weedy, crumbling places which is the nightmare of every kid on the block. Each room was a tomb, a vault, a mausoleum of lost love and unrelieved grief: the freezer of casseroles left over from the funeral, the untouched closets of my mother's clothes, bags of supplies from her office, her magazines, her used-up shampoos; we hadn't moved the tiniest thing, as if we feared even the dust would shift.

It was like the scrapbook I kept of her, which I'd put together after the funeral, pasting in the memorial-service announcement, the obituary, photographs. I'd been staring at it every night, as if I could conjure her love out of the sticky cardboard, and I only stopped when I finally realized I was pouring all my love into a book.

It was still two hours before I had to be at summer school, but I got dressed and left the house. I lingered at the newsstand by the subway, and there I saw it, gleaming at me from the cover of *Cosmopolitan*: "How to Find Love." I devoured it during my hour-long subway ride to school:

How to Find Love

Love may *happen* to some women—goddesses, movie stars, models—knights descend on them, scooping them onto white horses, hunks of the month call and ask them for dates. But the rest of us have to go out and *find our true loves.*

It isn't as hard as you think. He's out there, you just have to look for him. If you seem friendly and receptive, somebody attractive will get the message and start a conversation with you. So here's the secret to finding love: get out there, make yourself available, be open to love! Here are some places to start your search.

Libraries. Law, medical, university. Bring something to look up. Ask questions of male researchers: "How do I use this microfiche?"

In the supermarket. Look into his basket and ask where he got the fresh pesto. (Stay away from men with tampons in their carts—they have other interests.)

Be a hospital volunteer. A wealth of opportunities here: doctors, staff, patients—they do recover!

Car shows. Men flock to them...

"What the hell kind of guy are you gonna meet at a car show, someone from *Grease*? Danny Zucco? Kenickie?" a voice said over my shoulder. It was Kelsey Chun, my Spanish Level Two deskmate. I hadn't noticed when she'd gotten on the train, I'd been so engrossed in the article, and it was strange seeing her on the subway; I'd never seen her outside of school before. We were packed like sardines on the #7 train—mornings were always the worst, commuters scowling, grumbling in ten different languages, reaching desperately for the silver poles as the train squealed and tilted like it was about to topple off the tracks.

I smiled at her and stuffed the magazine into my bookbag, embarrassed to have been caught reading it. What if she thought I was desperate?

But I was desperate. I was always daydreaming, getting a crush on some guy—Luigi Bamboni, the cook at the Queens Burger, where I waitressed part-time; Richard Bridgewald, a doctor I met while my father was in the hospital; the list went on. During even the most awful day a crush could change everything, like a good-luck charm you took out and polished and revered, a jumping-off point for dreams and fantasies. Every new person I met, every crush I had, opened up reams of possibilities: people who could remove the world, who could fill in all of life's gaping holes.

And it wasn't so different with friendships: at Grand Central several passengers got up and we took their seats, and I loved the thought of it, riding the subway with Kelsey, walking the long blocks to school beside her. I stared at our reflections in the darkened window. My visions of friendship seemed no different from my crush fantasies—I wanted a best girlfriend as much as a boyfriend. In the first months after my mother died, my friends had seemed afraid to be with me, as if losing your mother was catching. Conversations hushed when I approached, eyes averted or else searched me with a horrified fascination, as if my mother's

death showed physically, like a huge wart or missing limb.

Those friendships had been hung on so little, I realized now, unlike the kind of best-friendship I imagined—someone who I could unburden my heart to wholly, in the dark, to sit beside at night and tell everything to. But was it a myth, that kind of friend? A myth like having a mother was a myth, or a father like the ones on TV?

Kelsey glanced at her watch. "How come you're going to school now? I've never seen you here before."

I shrugged. "I woke up early." I didn't want to say that it was my birthday, that I hadn't wanted to be home alone with my father. "What about you?"

"I usually get to school early to do homework—I never have time after school. I work at my parents' store or I make dinner for my stupid brothers or something. I'm a nerd now," she added with a resigned sigh, though with her sleek black hair and high-heeled boots she clearly wasn't. "I'm turning over a new leaf. You really just woke up early?" She looked at me oddly, as if she couldn't imagine a stranger thing to do.

"Well—it's actually…" Why not just say it? "It's my birthday."

Her eyes lit up. "Happy birthday! How old are you?"

"Sixteen."

"How are you celebrating? Are you having a sweet sixteen?"

"I don't think so." My father and I hadn't made any plans except for eating the Sara Lee cake in the freezer. "It's not such a big deal."

"It is," Kelsey said. "The last place you should be on your birthday is in school."

"That's true." High school was misery. Aside from the boring classes, the building itself was unbearable—desks bolted down, barred windows (did they think we'd steal the desks and jump out?), the soiled bathrooms, the cafeteria that smelled like cold oatmeal and cottage cheese. Then there were the people, guards who wouldn't let you in without your ID card, teachers taking attendance by ID number, the whole prisonlike, nameless, faceless state of being in public school.

At the Fifth Avenue station, we walked down the corridor to switch to the D train. "I know what we should do today," Kelsey said. "We should hang out in a supermarket and ask some guy where he got the pesto."

"Or we could saunter around a hospital, looking for cute patients," I said.

"I always wanted to be a candy striper."

"We should do it. We should stay out until we fall in love." I said it jokingly, but Kelsey raised her eyebrows in earnest.

"It is Friday," she said. "Neither of us has missed a day yet. Although not showing up is what got us into summer school in the first place."

I remembered the first day of class: Mrs. Torres had asked

why we'd failed Spanish during the regular year. I'd said, vaguely, because of an illness—not mentioning it had been my mother's—and Kelsey had answered that it was her appetite; she was always hungry. She was stick-thin, but she had a penchant for skipping class to find something good to eat.

I imagined it, the two of us off on our own, eating delicious things, roaming about the city, and it seemed more important than class or anything. "Have you ever been to Manhattan Bakery?" I said. "It's right near here. They have the best croissants in the city."

Before we could change our minds we were out on the street.

Businessmen marched up Fifth like a grey-tweed parade; we strode to the bakery and gazed at the pastries rising up like a hundred half-moons in the window. We bought two croissants and shared them in the park, digging our fingers into the soft buttery insides, puffs of cotton. How good they tasted, how good everything tastes when you're not supposed to be eating it, when right then we should've been saying *hola* to Mrs. Torres.

We wandered through Central Park and bought a romance novel at the Strand carts; at Sheep's Meadow we lay reading in the grass, skipping to the good parts, watching frisbees slice up the sun. Kelsey read aloud:

> Tristan reached his hand down to Anastasia's furry domain. He let it rest there, as the sensations swelled and swarmed through her tawny thighs and womanly petals…

"It's worse than *Cosmo*," I groaned.

She smiled. "My sister and I own more at home. Three shelves."

We saw a movie at the Paris Theater, with subtitles and a plot neither of us understood, and we walked across all of

Manhattan, through uptown, midtown, and downtown, to the Village, where we could shop.

Shopping: a girl's true cure for any ailment of the soul. It had begun to rain lightly, and we sauntered through the dampened Village streets, pausing in stores, admiring shop windows, buying earrings and barrettes from the umbrella-covered street vendors, sharing honey-roasted peanuts beneath an awning, the sweetness whirling out from the cart like a cloud. Years after I would still remember the sweet smell and softness of those peanuts in my mouth, almost melting, the warmth and satisfaction and escape from the damp.

We bought sleek black barrettes, the same kind, and silver rings with imitation rubies; we huddled under an umbrella and laughed at the crazy people walking by, muttering; we dipped our fingers into the peanut bag and clutched our packages by our sides.

And I realized, then, how with a new girl, just like with a boy, it's another kind of falling in love: I was enamored with her elegant stance, her effortless beauty, which she didn't even seem aware of; her easy laughter; her craziness, trying on a leopard-print bikini and three-foot-wide sombrero; the way her eyes darkened and widened as she spoke, and the circles underneath her eyes, like a sadness. And I think it was this sadness beneath, more than anything else, that made me know that I could love her.

We shared bits of ourselves in passing:

"My father sold gum on the streets of Seoul to put himself through college, and what was the fucking point of it, to own a goddamn store?"

"I wish my father'd reopen his shoe-repair shop and get off the fucking couch. I almost even miss the stories of everyone's smelly feet and bunions and corns..."

"This old Jewish man steals from us. Bread, stuffed in his shirt. My mother lets him, she feels sorry..."

"Oh my god, what if he's my father?"

Clutching our packages, we stopped in Roy Rogers for dinner. We loaded our buns up high and took them to the top section, all to ourselves. "We still haven't met our true loves," she said.

I glanced at my watch. "I think the libraries are closed." It was already five o'clock; my father was probably home on the couch, ready to tell me how his grilled chicken was.

"Do you have to be home a certain time?"

"No," I said, thinking of the Sara Lee cake in the freezer. We hadn't made any specific plans for when we'd eat it; it was surely still frozen rock-hard in its foil pan. My father never made any rules for what time I had to come home, unlike my mother, who always stayed awake worrying, waiting for me to return. I'd hardly gone out since she died, and the few times I had he hadn't waited up, but I didn't want him to start now. "Maybe I should call him," I said.

I fished out a quarter and used the payphone by the entrance. "Daddy? It's Mia. I'm out with my friend Kelsey. I think I'm going to be home a little late, okay?"

I half-expected him, like my mother had, to launch into a barrage of questions—wanting the full itinerary, with phone numbers, addresses, exact longitudes of where I'd be—but he didn't. He told me happy birthday, and then said, "You're missing *Picket Fences*."

"Yeah, well. You can tell me what happened."

"I don't know if I'll remember," he yawned, and told me to have a good time, and we hung up.

Back at the table I asked Kelsey, "What about you? Do you have to call your parents?"

She shook her head. "They keep the store open till midnight; usually they don't get home till one. I never even see them. I could stay out all night and they wouldn't notice—

it's fine as long as I don't wake them up, barging in at three."
She smiled. "Let's do that—let's stay out all night."
I nodded. "Until our womanly petals bloom."

We didn't have to enter a hospital, a supermarket, or a car show; we only had to sit in 10th Street Bar for fifteen minutes before two men sat down. Miraculous, I thought.

"You must be a wonderful Spanish teacher," Perry was saying to Kelsey. Perry and Corky: Corky was mine. They sounded like the names of goldfish, but they were handsome, gorgeous—they were men. They were from London, soccer players, coaching at a camp in Connecticut, in the city for the night

Kelsey laughed delightedly. She'd clearly done this before; she'd said we'd have no problem sneaking in, they never carded. And she was right, and the two men were swallowing her stories as eagerly as their drinks: she was a Spanish teacher at a high school, she'd told them, and, staring into her Black Bunny beer, explained that I was studying to be a vet.

I'd sipped half my gin and tonic but already I could feel it. "Ready for another?" Corky asked.

I shook my head. "Work tomorrow," I said gravely.

"Veterinary medicine—I imagine that must be a rewarding profession."

"Oh, it is. You get that sick bunny on the examining table and—oh, it's rewarding."

What the hell were we doing? It was thrilling, exciting (Were these men really taking us seriously? Could they really be interested in us?) but it also made me feel a little ill, and frightened, as if we were crossing over into territory I wanted to enter, but wasn't sure how. Earlier, in Central Park, Kelsey and I'd mutually confessed our virginities, and agreed we'd wait until we fell in love. This wasn't love, with these men, that much was clear, but it was intimidating just the same. It was one thing to read romance novels, and another to have the physical fact of a man right there, itching to get into your furry domain.

"Have you been in class all day?" Perry asked.

"No," Kelsey said. "We've been celebrating Mia's twenty-second birthday. *Feliz Cumpleaños!*"

She and Perry raised their glasses, and Corky bought me another drink. The clock ticked away, midnight, one. Kelsey told them about lying in Sheep's Meadow, and the movie, and shopping, as if we'd been friends for years.

"Do you do this on your birthday every year? Make it a full holiday?" Corky asked me.

"Kind of," I said, and for the first time I thought of my previous birthday, before my mother got sick. She'd bought me half a cake from a gourmet shop in Manhattan, because she didn't have time to make one, and she figured we never ate the whole thing anyway. She'd placed it on the table and I'd peered around it, looking for the other half. "What happened? Did you get hungry?" I'd asked her, and she'd shaken her head and blushed, saying it was expensive, she'd thought half seemed like a better idea. I'd sulked, feeling sorry for my measly half-cake, and, oh, I could kill myself now for not appreciating it then. Now I'd jump into her lap and hug her and savor every single bite, and why had it seemed so imperfect then?

And why, in the morning when I'd awoken, had my memories of past birthdays been so sugar coated, why had I not thought of the less-than-perfect ones too? And even more frightening was the way these memories still haunted me, dredging themselves up, unwarranted, constantly poking through—remember me, remember me—when I didn't want to remember any of them; I didn't.

I stared at the floor. Tears brimmed in my eyes and I blinked them back, but they poured out anyway; I cried into my drink. This always happened. It was pathetic, I was a professional weeper; if they had a course in it at school I'd excel for once. I cried on every holiday, on Mother's Day, her birthday, and the twenty-sixth of every month, the anniversary of her death.

Corky looked horrified; he stood back. "What's wrong?"

I shook my head.

"What's up with her?" Perry asked Kelsey, as if I were some kind of freak. Kelsey didn't answer; she put her hand on my shoulder and waited for me to stop crying, which I didn't. We went to the bathroom for tissue, and when we came out the two men had left.

We sat on the wooden bench in the subway station, waiting for the #7 train to take us home. "Why did you do that?" Kelsey asked. "Why did you start crying?"

I shrugged. We hadn't spoken since we'd left the bar. I looked around the station. It was surprisingly packed, but only with men. A big, toothless man paced by us back and forth, leering like he was hungry and we were lunch. Perhaps we're just going to die, I thought, and at two A.M. this began to sound good: then I'd see my mother.

I stared at the tracks. "I don't know."

After a few moments she said, "Where's your mother? You've never talked about her."

My heart jumped, as it did whenever anybody asked; each time it was still a surprise. I shrugged. I looked down at the floor. Scuff on my black shoes. Snickers wrapper. Discarded gum. She's in the cemetery. Decomposing, I once thought to say. But I said the usual, "She died in January," as if giving the month made it real. It didn't. Seven months had passed and here I was, the words still crumbled into me, hollow breaking lumps, screws in the chest, neverending.

"I'm sorry."

She didn't say anything else, she just looked at me, but not in the odd, surprised way—she looked at me plainly, like she was taking me in. Like she was waiting for me to say something more. And that plainness surprised me, that open vast simplicity of her face, and I stared back at my shoes, the dirty floor. What purpose was it, all the crying, the heartbreak? I ruined our chances with those guys, I ruined our perfect day, I ruined love.

"I'm sorry I made those guys run off," I sniffed.

"They were creeps—I'm glad you did."

I wiped my nose on my sleeve; a few latent sobs were still working their way out.

"I've cried in the worst places, too," she said quietly, as the train finally pulled into the station. "When my parents first opened the store, I cried nearly every day. I couldn't understand why they were working such long hours; I thought each morning when they left that they were never coming back."

"But you were like six, or seven."

She shrugged. "It doesn't matter."

I sniffed again. "I'm still sorry. It's been seven months. I should be over it by now."

"No you shouldn't," she said.

At Queensborough Plaza, three stops before my house and six before hers, Kelsey checked her watch. "It's almost two. My parents'll kill me if I come home now and wake them up. Do you mind—can I stay at your house?"

"Oh, sure," I croaked, horror rising up in my throat at the idea. How could I bring her to Spooky House? But I didn't have a choice; I couldn't say no. I braced myself during the rest of the ride, and cringed as we walked the three long blocks from the subway to my house, past the weeds, the slanting trees, the overgrown roots cracking up the sidewalk, the peeling paint on our red stoop. That stoop I'd played on, hiked up jauntily so many years, and now dreaded, loathed, winced to even look at.

I drew in my breath as we entered our dark living room. Pillows and newspapers were strewn on the floor; dirty mugs, plates, and the partly eaten Sara Lee cake cluttered the coffee table. My father was asleep on the couch in his sweatpants and undershirt; he woke up and blinked at us when I shut the door. For a moment he seemed alarmed, and then confused, and then he just looked awkward, and I wondered if he was thinking, oh, now she brings a friend over, at last, at two-thirty in the morning.

He pulled his button-down shirt off the chair and buttoned it off-kilter, so it hung about him loosely, like a tablecloth. He hadn't shaved in days. There was dried ketchup on the pocket of his shirt. The hair he usually brushed over his bald spot hung down one side of his face, like a new-wave haircut. I told him we were at a party that ended late, and introduced them to each other.

"You'd like some coffee, Leslie?" my father said.

"Kelsey," I said.

"Kell-see. Kell-see. A slice of cake? Skim milk?"

I shook my head. "Maybe in the morning. I'm sorry. We're really tired."

But Kelsey was eyeing the chocolate cake. "I'd love a slice," she said.

So the three of us sat there, on our living-room couch, drinking skim milk, and eating birthday cake (it was still partly frozen in the middle) off yellow napkins imprinted with *Wendy's*. My father pulled my birthday presents out of a grocery bag beneath the table; they were wrapped in newspaper and tied with a bow of string.

"Oh, wow," I said, tearing off the paper, "Teen Lady. I love them." My father seemed pleased; we said goodnight and I led Kelsey upstairs to my room, all the time waiting for her to revolt, to refuse to be with me any longer in my crazy, decrepit house.

I opened the door to my room—the old single bed, the felt giraffe on the wall. I hated it, our frozen house, my stupid childhood room, which I'd never changed, redecorated; I was never able to part with a fucking thing. I thought we'd go to bed quickly: I gave her a toothbrush, nightgown, towel, and turned down the sheets, but she didn't seem ready to sleep.

The scrapbook, the one of my mother, the one I'd resolved to stop looking at, lay on the shelf beside my bed; she picked it up. Quilted cover, photos pasted in. My heart flinched to watch her open it: there were my insides, spilling out—this naked love on the page. I was embarrassed to show it, this raw, doting, unharnessed outpouring. My mother, in every period of her life, and every year of mine. Ridiculous things, I'd pasted in there: not just the birthday cards and postcards, volumes of them—that might be all right, but I'd included doodles on a telephone pad, a price tag from a dress we'd bought together, her signature on a credit-card receipt, a grocery list I'd found in her pocketbook with just three words: *bread, milk, chocolate.*

Kelsey fingered the plastic sheets, touching it all.

"You're lucky," she said. "You're lucky to have had her."

I stared at her. It was the first time anyone had ever said that to me.

She lay back in bed, and we stared up at the shapes in the peeled-off plaster of the ceiling. There was something between us in the air; something tangible, real. I had cried, the men had left, my father had served us cake which was still frozen in the middle—but at the end of the day, we were lying here together, in the quiet, the edge of her warm nightgown touching mine, and I thought that this was what she meant by lucky: simply this. 🏃

Siobhan Dowd of International PEN's Writers-in-Prison Committee in London writes this column regularly, alerting readers to the plight of writers around the world who deserve our awareness and our writing action.

Writer Detained: Flora Brovina
by Siobhan Dowd

*I*t may take years to pick up the pieces in Kosovo, and for now the possibility of Kosovan Serbs and Albanians living amicably side by side seems remote. But before the situation spiralled into the all-out conflict of NATO bombing, mass graves, and flight by all parties in all directions, a few sane voices did plead for a solution that avoided the carnage. Flora Brovina, an Albanian writer currently under arrest in Serb territory, was one of them.

A fifty-year-old poet, women's activist, and pediatrician, Brovina is an Albanian who has denounced Serb human-rights abuses in Kosovo, called for independence for the region, but also wanted, throughout, a non-violent approach. Her poems are extremely popular in the region and she has published four books. She is on record as having stated in January that "if this war is not stopped it will get much bigger. It will be worse than Bosnia." In March last year she was one of the organizers of a march of twenty thousand ethnic Albanian women whose message was unambiguous: "Peace." They gathered near the United States Center of Information in Pristina, waving sheets of blank, white paper. She explains that the paper symbolized their belief that "All options were still open" and "Nothing had been written down." There was still time to broker a peace that would allow ethnic Albanians the right to self-determination, grant Kosovo back its autonomy, and put an end to a Serb military dominance in the region that had become increasingly ugly.

Brovina has worked as a doctor for many years in Pristina. After the regime of President Milosevic revoked Kosovo's technical status as an autonomous republic, the Kosovan Liberation Army grew, drawing its members mainly from rural areas. The Serb army marched into the region to counter the emerging revolutionaries, and very quickly reports of atrocities began emerging. Albanian intellectuals in key jobs found themselves fired—including Brovina, who was dismissed from her post at a Pristina hospital. Her involvement in the ensuing struggle was prompted by a massacre in Likosane, a small village in central Kosovo: "I saw pictures of an entire family that had been slaughtered," she said. "I saw helpless children who had been gunned down." She founded and became president of The Women's League of Kosovo, a movement that organized peaceful demonstrations and mobilized mass support against the violence. In October 1998, she participated in a student protest that was broken up by police with baton charges and tear gas. "They beat me on the back with a baton," she recalled later. "And I still didn't leave." She also established a clinic and refuge for women and children in Pristina. Its emphasis was on disseminating basic health education. Leaflets were produced aimed at helping families through critical times, with advice ranging from treating snake bites and dressing wounds to delivering babies. An orphanage was also set up for children who had lost their parents to the civil war, containing up to twenty-five children at any one time. (When the Albanians reclaimed Pristina, the orphanage was found deserted. Nobody knows what happened to the children.)

As the NATO bombing began, Brovina's husband, who had been in Belgrade on business, fled to Tirana. Brovina herself opted to stay in Pristina, and not flee, believing that her medical skills would be needed. She moved to a neighbor's house, hoping thereby to avoid the notice of the Serb forces, and kept a diary of events on a wad of graph paper. She records visits to pregnant women and clinic sessions conducted amid a city falling apart at the seams. The last entry she wrote, found after the Serb forces withdrew, was on March 26. "I came here at 11:25. Nobody in the streets. People are waiting for bread—long lines. Telephone disconnected—even here. Now I don't have any connection with anyone."

The first news of her arrest broke on April 24, when Brovina's son e-mailed the writers' association PEN. He reported that she had been picked up two days earlier by what he termed "Serb masked paramilitaries" who lay in wait for her where she was staying and took her away in a car. He urgently requested that the news be disseminated as widely as possible. For some time, her whereabouts remained unknown; there were fears for her life. However, it was discovered that she was alive, and held in a prison near Pristina. As the Serb troops, however, withdrew from the region, she was among hundreds of detainees transferred to a prison in Pozarevac in Serbia.

A *Washington Post* staff writer reported that visitors there in July found her pale but defiant. With her boots missing their laces, she stood with her hands clasped behind her back and trounced the Serbian criminal-justice system—despite the fact that two disapproving wardens were looking on. She said that she was not a prisoner so much as a "bargaining chip." She has been charged with being a terrorist—specifically with "joining in enemy duties" and engaging in "criminal acts endangering the territorial integrity" of the state. The charges appear to be linked solely to her many humanitarian activities and gestures of peaceful protest. Her husband, who has now returned to Pristina, says that her high blood pressure has been exacerbated by her imprisonment. There are fears that if she is not released soon, her health will deteriorate further.

Please write polite letters appealing for Flora Brovina to be released to:

His Excellency Slobodan Milosevic
President of Yugoslavia
Savezna Skupstina
11000 Belgrade
Federal Republic of Yugoslavia
Fax: 011 381 11636 775

Manuel Muñoz

*An unfortunately damaged photo, but my sister Elisa
and I never looked sharper, in the late seventies,
dressed to the "nueves" by our grandmother and mom.
A floral-patterned collar, and butterfly at that.*

Manuel Muñoz received an MFA in fiction from Cornell. His work has appeared in the *Mid-American Review* and the Chicano Chapbook Series. He was awarded a writing grant from the Constance Saltonstall Foundation for the Arts, and has completed a novel, *The Stormed House*.

MANUEL MUÑOZ
Campo

Just at the base of the foothills, the town levels a space for itself between the vineyards of summer raisins and the fruit orchards. Though some of the workers live in this town, it is mostly a place for wide, open-porched houses, white wood, painted just this past spring. The lawns look even greener because of the shade of Chinese elms, though most of the trees shed a dusty fungus from their leaves so that, by September, they'll have released too early. The streets run diagonal in places, the intersections in town meeting in curious six-way stops, small islands of parks dotting the gaps where the streets miss each other.

The women who live in these houses, while their men are away, spend their time browsing the downtown shops. Many like to visit the sewing-and-crafts store in particular, located on a choice corner of downtown and owned by a woman who lives in a bigger house than they do—she tends a porch that skirts all the way around the home, the floorboards painted grey, the rails flower-lined. She sells them ribbon, fabric, and picture frames handmade from nectarine wood. Because it is summer, she displays a long skirt that she made, modeled by the headless mannequin in her window. The women in town stop to admire the white, almost sheer cloth, and the brilliant, delicately small orange poppies that pepper the fabric.

The workers, though, do not live close to downtown. Past the county courthouse, with its palm-lined lawn and arc of black gate, the main road continues, and then blanches away to a crumbling, thinner passage. It travels past the gasoline tanks and the giant cooling sheds of the ice company. Past these structures, away from the sight of the rest of the town, is the workers' neighborhood. They can walk to town and often do, past the courthouse, past the window with the primped mannequin, to get groceries, about twenty minutes each way. Mostly it is the wives who go, followed by shirtless children, and then return again. There is a park across the road from the county courthouse—the last nicely kept park before the gasoline tanks and the ice company—and here people stop if they are walking, to rest in the grass, just for a few minutes, because they carry perishables off both arms.

It was only at the beginning of summer that the labor camp—off an even more vague strip of road than the one that began to falter after the county courthouse—was started up again. Hidden from view of the road by a nest of nectarine trees, the changing light of early evening brought the first signs that the camp was back in operation. At the workers' park, when the grass cooled and people relaxed, ribbons of smoke rose from the direction of the camp. The workers who had lived in this town many years assured the rest that the smoke was not a house on fire, or a rancher burning weeds, or kids lighting abandoned tires.

The camp, they told the rest, had not been used in years, the owner of it having died some time back. The mayor and the town council had gone out there personally, week after week, once the owner had passed away, and arrested workers who tried to live there free of charge. The owner, they claimed, had left no relatives his land, had left no one to oversee the cleanliness and operation of the skinny cabins in the trees. His bright yellow ranch house and twenty-six horses he left all alone and to no one. At the public auction, some workers pulled together their money to buy oak tables and a washing machine, and they carted home all the tools that had been rusting in his shed since long before he died.

For several evenings, the workers at the park lounge in the grass, call out hello to those coming and going to town. At this hour, it is usually men going to buy beer. The married ones have gone home to eat and the smoke from the camp rises almost at the dot of what would be a dinner hour. But these men crack open sunflower seeds and spit the husks in the grass. They are far from home and have no one to cook for them.

It is on a Sunday that they first see the teenage boy, followed by a thread of children, too many to count as they run at each other and into the street. The boy is tall, hair as dark as theirs, but his skin is too light for this time of year, and they guess that he is not a worker, or that he might be ill. For a boy of his height, his slender build makes him seem dangerously thin, and he walks as if bent at the waist, having been dealt a blow. He rings around the children, placing his hands on their backs to keep them from straying into the road and, as this is Sunday and the workers are not working, there are more cars on the road than usual. Without saying hello to him, the workers watch the thin boy as he passes the park, and observe that there are three children who obey him, walk patiently next to him, hold out their hands as if to reaffirm that they are the best behaved and need to be told as much.

Some of those children don't have shoes, says one of the workers, and it's this that makes them believe that the boy has come from the camp, with this line of children.

Because he is tall, the boy believes the children will obey him, and they do, though some of the smaller children give him trouble. At the camp, during the day, he does not allow any of them to run off for the afternoon until their chores are done, and he brings together all fifteen of the children, circled around him, his eyes on the ones who turn their heads to the orchard and its temptations.

Having no choice, he chooses the most responsible children and commands the rest of them to obey, but, knowing this will not happen, he runs quickly from each cabin, surveying, helping with the sweep of the floor, the pick-up of the garbage piled in the corners. One little girl is sidetracked by a naked doll, its hair clumped with twigs and mud, and he takes it from her and raises it above her head, tells the rest that they will play soon, taking turns washing the doll in a basin.

He finds this duty worrisome, his body always tired. At night, he must wait until all the children are asleep, which takes a while, because some of the older boys want to sleep all by themselves in the empty cabins. But he tells them that this is not possible, that they must sleep in their allotted spots.

On the way to town, he wonders about how he will manage to keep the smaller children away from the candy shelves and the toys, what he might use to appease them. He wishes that his pockets were full of trinkets or pieces of gum, so that he might bribe them still.

There is a woman in town who owns a smooth-running car, the whole front seat a bench that runs undivided from door to door. She closes her windows to the heat of the day and turns the air conditioning on low, so as not to waste fuel. Her husband does not attend the Methodist church with her, so it is her hat which occupies the seat. Later in the evening, as they always do on Sundays, her husband will take the wheel and they will drive the outskirts of town. It is not so hot then, so they'll not need the air conditioning.

At an intersection, though she has clearance, she chooses to wait for a group of children approaching in a haggard line. Her car idles as she watches the children cross in front of her automobile, several of them barefoot and tiptoeing with painful grimaces across the hot asphalt, some of them wise enough to use the cooler, painted yellow lines.

Before services begin, she asks several of her women friends if they have seen these children. One woman, wearing a scarf made of the sheer white cloth with the poppies, remarks that it is not surprising. Another says that the county should come have a look, but it is Sunday, so nothing can be done.

All through services, the woman thinks of those children, at times angry, at times sad. She thinks of her husband at home reading the morning edition, his loafers resting against the rug; her two sons, gone now, never without shoes, even in the summertime, when prickthorns sprouted in even the best of lawns.

Several women attend the afternoon tea arranged by the owner of the sewing-and-crafts store. Around the length of porch, talk turns to the barefoot children, and the car-owning woman nods now and then with self-assurance as questions are asked of her. She nibbles the cookies set out by the hostess, sips the sun-brewed tea, tells again what she has seen.

The boy finds that he is the one distracted when he leads the children through downtown. He tries to keep his mind on the pound of ground beef he'll need to bring home in brown paper and the milk and which of the bigger boys will carry the five-pound bag of potatoes. But the record shop tempts him to look. It caters to the workers via a small megaphone playing songs in tinny voices. Even so, he recognizes the places those singers come from, their faces smiling at him from the posters taped crookedly to the windows.

He makes the children file past the open door, remembering the bustle of Sunday cars, ordering the holding of hands,
the smallest hand in his. At the sewing store, as they wait for a
light, the boy ignores the traffic and stares at the white dress
with orange poppies, flowers he recalls seeing outside of
Bakersfield, on the way north. It had been dusty and, after so
many cotton fields, the sides of the road had suddenly
bloomed in these same tiny flowers, and everyone in the
truck had looked at them and pointed.

He sees the clean lines of the dress, how it must be handmade because of the stitching, the bolt of the same fabric
tossed leisurely at the foot of the mannequin. The boy
wonders who in town could wear such a beautiful dress, and
where, and why, and who would take them.

When the small hand in his tugs hard, the boy finds himself
surrounded by the children pressing their faces into the glass,
leaving oily smudges. He tells them to stop it, to pull away,
and then bends down to rub clean the smears with the hem
of his shirt, leaving the window as spotless as when they first
walked by.

There is another boy, also young, a worker, who lives with
some of the other men in a two-bedroom house right next to
the ice company. Sleeping on the floor of the front room, the
noise from the ice-company coolers keeps him awake at
night, as workers are always opening and closing wide steel
doors and shifting forklifts loaded with pallets of frozen fruit.

This boy has trusted the other men with his last ten dollars,
remaining in the park by himself while the rest go to buy
beer. He stays behind in the idle park hoping to see the boy
with the children, because he wonders why he is entrusted
with so many little hands and feet. He believes that the boy,
like him, stays awake at night to the sound of the kids playing,
and that he must go, the way he does himself, tired through

the day and restless because he has no rest.

When he spots them, he sees that the boy is carrying all four of the paper bags and the children follow along behind him quickly, as if he has only just scolded them and they are still scared enough to follow orders. From this distance, he can see the boy's face glisten with sweat, and he wants to shout to him or raise his hand.

It is when that boy and his children are directly across the street that he does not think and runs across, darting between the Sunday cars. He hears the men, returning with the beer, yelling from down the street—what is he doing, where might he be going—and he feels caught, the boy looking at him strangely and quickening his pace, clutching the bags. The beer men keep shouting at him and he tries to ask the boy his name, where he's from, and why, but the children surge forward, carrying him off before he can make an answer. For a moment he is left alone, the boy and the children rapidly departing, the others catcalling their questions.

At night the boy cannot sleep, though he has tired the children with a game of hide-and-seek in the orchard. The children ran among the trees, climbing in them, losing themselves for a good long time before some started throwing the fruit which lay rotting in the soil, and he ordered the game over.

When he closes his eyes, he can only picture the young man at the park, dashing across the road as if he had something urgent to tell him. He remembers him as a frenetic force, his legs pumping across the road, shirtless, worked, deep dark from his face to his belly button. He had stood close enough to know that he was taller, and the proximity, the brute presence of him, alarmed the boy, made him open his eyes once more in the dark. And when he tried to sleep, it was again the round, dark face, the hair pushed back and not cut cleanly, the eyes oddly green. He blends him with the postered faces in the record shop, the eyes beginning to fade and yellow from so much sun, the music coming from a dark interior.

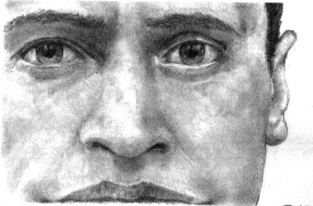

J. Olson 99 -

The boy in the park is again at the park, though it is Monday, and afternoon. The grass around him is spare and no one is off work yet, but he understands that he is not like the workers around him. They all drink Budweiser or Coors from cans, wear white T-shirts that come in packages, are dark from work, do not smoke because they would rather drink. Some are from other places, some are brothers and cousins. Some work in the morning, others are like the workers for the ice company, keeping awake during the short summer nights with coffee and triple cigarette breaks.

He is a young worker and cannot stand up for an entire day's work, and the other men know it and send him home to eat before he collapses on them, the way he did during the early summer, tumbling from a ladder while picking plums, spilling the fruit, which the other men scurried to hide from the foreman. He is known to be weak.

On his way home, he had to walk the mile and a half from the farm to the park, past the lane which leads to the camp, the cabins a circle in the trees. Resisting the urge to follow the dirt lane, he thought of cornered rabbits, the way they kept still when he approached them hidden in the grass patches between plum trees, and the feeling of the bones and fur in his hands when he picked them up, their hind legs kicking, the heart rapid, straight to his palm.

The boy is awake before the sun rises and it is quiet, the children around him so still for once. Down the lane, the taillights of trucks blink red as they move along the road, wink in the spaces between the trees. It is dark enough still to feel that it is night, that it is too early for anyone but workers to rise and begin the day.

But the boy is awake because he has not slept, and he closes his eyes to try, because the children will wake soon and not tire from running and not listening. He wonders if the end of the day will bring the end of his caring for them, if he'll be allowed to move on as he pleases, because he is older and can care for himself.

Of the children, he feels the most pity for the little girls, for they will be held close long after they will want to leave these lives. But the boys—as they do already with their claiming of the empty cabins, with the manner in which they scamper through the trees and feel no need to tell him where they are—they will go on without anyone.

The boy shifts to lie on his back and he puts his hands behind his head, so that he can see the sky through the holes of the cabin roof. It is lightening slowly, and within the hour the children will surely be stirred by it. He closes against it, and remembers the deserts of Arizona, the strange coolness of Washington, though it was summer and the strawberries hung rich on the ground. He knows that places are not what they are after a matter of months. Workers have told him of the monsoon rains that turn the Arizona sand to a silky mud, and he himself was already moving south when they finished the strawberries, and the wind, said a man at a gas station, was too cold for that time of year.

He jumps from sleep because he has thought of the boy who ran to him, found himself wondering where the boy came from and what kept him here. When he opens his eyes the sky is brighter, but the children have not moved, so the boy rises and steps out. At this time of day, the morning air is almost chilly, enough to wake anyone up without the need to splash water on the face, so he stands and lets his arms goosebump and folds them against his chest. Off on the road, the cars and trucks are making much more noise because day has arrived, and the boy does not stop himself from wondering, under the wide sky and awake, about the running boy and the whys and wheres and hows of him. He thinks of the places that boy has been, if there are ones he would like to visit again, if someone gave him the permission to follow the direction he thought fit best.

He is watching the skyline above the camp, though there would not be smoke at this time of day. The slamming of car doors finally turns him to the county courthouse, where now inches a full line of cars into parking spaces and several women stand near the palm trees, some holding purses, looking at the closed doors of the front office. So many of them are wearing some form of white that it takes him a moment to realize that their skirts or light scarves or headbands are not white, but dotted. They all seem to move in unison, pitching their ears toward the courthouse walls as if, collectively, they might be able to hear and know what is being discussed inside.

It is curious to him, and he keeps watching, because there is still no smoke at the camp skyline. And finally, as if the women have known that he has been suspicious of them, they move suddenly into their automobiles, gunning their motors, turning their cars to follow a county sedan, a large green star painted on the side, leaving from the backlot of the courthouse.

Instantly, because he knows where the green-star car is headed, and where the women intend to follow, the boy bolts down the street after them, running hard and feeling the fatigue almost as soon as he starts. His heels strike the hard pavement and then have trouble gripping as the asphalt fades out to the thinner surface, the gravel too loose in places. Up ahead the cars have turned, in succession, in the direction of the camp.

The boy runs through the orchards instead, across the uneven furrows, his feet dashing apart fallen fruit, small animals scurrying away from his presence. There are workers in the midst of trees and they shout to him that he is crazy, or that he should climb a ladder and pick plums just as fast, but he runs on, not knowing now where the cars might be, or if the boy and the children are there, if he might intercept them.

He had not started lunch yet because he had set the children to cleaning the cabins, and then refused to feed them when many of them fled into the orchards to play hide-and-seek again. They came complaining of hunger, and the smaller ones had succumbed to too much fruit and hunched with dropped pants behind the main quarters.

It is in the middle of cooking the ground beef and potatoes that the boy hears the rumble of cars. In the kickup of dust, one pulls ahead of the rest and stops. He hears the crackle of a radio relaying a message, and then a man in a beige uniform steps from the car and speaks back into the radio, looking at him and the children while he does so.

He is calm when the man approaches; he tries to gather the children who are not ill from fruit, wonders whether or not to put out the fire for lunch. The man in the beige uniform says something to him that he cannot understand, and the boy sees that he will not be able to explain, make the man understand that the mothers and fathers will be arriving any day now and wondering, that they all might miss each other as they head back south on the highway, the bordering fields holding the orange poppies.

He is trying to clutch as many of the children as he can, but his arms feel small. The beige-uniform man keeps speaking to him, though he knows it is futile. From the other cars, the boy sees, one by one, women emerging, wearing white, so brilliant in the heat of the afternoon against the green of the orchard and the dusty lane.

The beige-uniform man motions them all still and goes back to his car, where he speaks confidently into his radio. He opens his trunk and brings out a black bag and then walks over, opening it along the way and removing small wooden sticks. He counts the children in his quiet tongue and then draws the youngest one to him, who begins to cry, but the boy tells her to be still as the man pushes the wooden stick through her hair, searching.

The boy waits. The wide space around the cabins is crowded by the presence of this man. The women in white want to draw closer, he can tell, because some of them twist their heads forward, walk towards the cabins, and then hesitate. He brings each child back to him—how small they are—when the man is finished with them, and holds them tight and pleads with them to listen, though he knows they are too frightened to do otherwise.

From the edge of the orchard, he sees the boy from yesterday emerge, breathless and sweating, his shirt removed, and the women's calls of attention turn the man around to see him. With authority, the man barks at him to come closer, and the boy from yesterday hesitates, but approaches.

The boy holds the children's shoulders and the man, with difficulty, finally uses his fingers to ask if they are together, if they are one. He brings one finger to the other and pairs them, twists them together and locks them, looking at each boy to see the answer, does it again because neither responds.

It is the boy from yesterday that nods his head yes; he points at him and claims him to the man in the beige uniform who cannot understand. He hears the boy from yesterday speak, and the words, though rough and chopped, inform the man enough to ask more questions. The boy from yesterday answers again, pulls out money from his pockets as if this is to take care of them, edging closer and closer to the group, so close.

The boy cannot grip the children any harder. He can see the eyes again and the hair that was cut too long ago, the sweat collecting in beads across the chest, the flashing teeth. The arms begin to tell the story as well, the man in the uniform seeming to understand, and the boy does not know what to do, because he does not know what the boy from yesterday wants, what he believes, and is frightened to find out. He tries No to the man in the uniform, but the man has stopped looking at him. No, he tries again, and there is a moan from the back of their cabin, and the sick children cry out that they are sicker. The man in the uniform seems to grimace at the nuisance of it and then, reluctantly, turns to the women for help.

The boy watches them come, the white dresses and their sudden, orange poppies flowering with the closed distance. The man writes in a black leather booklet and he can hear the pen as it scribbles across the paper. Next to him, the boy from yesterday stands so near now that he can smell his copper scent, and when the green eyes look at him, he does not want to know any longer what it is like to be so close to things. 🕴

Roland Sodowsky

Brand-new striped overalls: Is this it? Is there
anything else one could possibly want in life?

Roland Sodowsky grew up on a small ranch in western Oklahoma. He
teaches creative writing, literature, and fiction-theory courses at Southwest
Missouri State University, Springfield, Missouri. His books include the
Associated Writing Program's 1988 short-fiction award-winner *Things We
Lose* (U. Missouri Press, 1989), *Interim in the Desert* (TCU Press, 1990), and
Undue West (Corona Press, 1990). His work has appeared in *Atlantic Monthly*,
Epoch, and *Studies in Short Fiction*, among many others. He received the
Coordinating Council of Literary Magazines' award for fiction in 1984, a
National Endowment for the Arts fiction grant in 1989, and the National
Cowboy Hall of Fame award for short fiction in 1991. He served as fiction
co-editor of *Short Story*, a literary magazine, from 1991 to 1995.

ROLAND SODOWSKY
What We Have to, What We Can

*N*othing but head and a blur: there's efficiency. Brain and eyes, needle beak, and blur. Not even that: here, over there. Gone. Back. And you didn't see him come or go.

If you could sell cars like that. Handle deals like that.

Wayman Dvorak wasn't actually standing at the kitchen sink as he thought about the dark green hummingbird that fed so voraciously through the yellow plastic petals on the red feeder outside the kitchen window. His daughter Elizabeth had given him the feeder on his forty-first birthday. It had sat on a shelf in the garage for a year and a half, until she complained that spring. So he had hung it near the fancy wren house Sally in accounting had given him, first asking Sally how to cook up the fake nectar, one part sugar to four parts boiling water. To his surprise, a hummingbird appeared immediately and had fed all summer, darting and banging angrily at the feeder when Wayman forgot to refill it. The tiny dynamo, its head incongruously large, its underside a pale, creamy grey, had a nest in the back-fence neighbor's yard, either in the trumpet vine or the sweetgum tree above it.

Wayman was in the bedroom dressing, his combed hair still wet from the shower. He checked the collar of one of his eight white shirts—still okay—put it on and buttoned it slowly. On the bed before him, Willa sighed raggedly and flopped from her right to left side, bunching the covers under her. She slammed her forearm down exactly where, Wayman calculated, his lowermost ribs would have been an hour earlier. She resumed her sleeping rhythm immediately, her outflung arm drawing back toward her until her hand, loosely fisted, rested on her hair. Her short, practically GI haircut, he thought, a little bitterly—shaded now to the oranginess of a ripening tomato—tapered to nothing behind her ears, far too high on her neck. His memory of the luxury of her hair, a few grey strands among the brown profusion, not light or dark and certainly not dyed, like summer curtains over her breasts, was fading.

For all his married life, this had been the best hour of the day. It began at the kitchen window while he drank coffee—neither cream nor sugar now—and ate his cereal and toast or a bagel and steamed wiener. Three years ago, the same year Willa had started back to school full time, Elizabeth, who had been thirteen then, had given him a little frankfurter cooker for Christmas. It looked like junk, but it steamed a wiener to sweaty, bursting perfection in an amazingly short time. To Willa's disgust, Wayman began eating an onion bagel and a wiener, with a good-sized dollop of brown mustard, every Tuesday and Thursday morning.

"For breakfast," Willa had said as she stuffed books and granola bars in her backpack. She had a morning class that winter. "Nevermind that you eat standing up. Nevermind that we know more about animal fat and cholesterol and sodium than ever before. But for *breakfast*."

"Just twice a week." He had held out the half-eaten bagel sandwich. "Try it, it's good."

"Thanks but no thanks," she said, and a few seconds later her Geo zipped out of the carport. She had taken to backing it in, like a fire truck ready for an emergency. When Wayman had said that once, jokingly, to Elizabeth, she answered, "Or to run from us. Maybe that's the emergency."

The best hour of the day: in the kitchen watching the robins and doves and a rowdy outlaw squirrel in the backyard, and now the hummingbird too, then dressing at the foot of the bed, with Willa there. Her face was relaxed, gentler in sleep, her lips still so puckerish and kissable, like those Precious Moments things his mother collected, that he was embarrassed to think about it. Mostly he just liked her presence, enjoyed his awareness of it, while his mind bumped around, happy as a Labrador pup. Sometimes he thought about Geos or Cadillacs or Subarus, or commissions, but usually not.

It had been there earlier as Wayman ate his shredded wheat. How it hovered, its pin-thin legs drawn up out of sight, eyes focused on the center of the yellow target, beak poised! That concentration: confident as a salesman folding a signed contract.

Wayman buttoned the cuffs of his shirt. The semester Willa enrolled in school, she had come back from the mall one Sunday afternoon and tossed an armful of new white dress shirts on the bed.

"Eight of them," she said. "One for every workday, and your days off if you fill in for someone, one more if they don't get washed till Monday night. All easy-care. If you hang them right out of the dryer, there won't be a single wrinkle. I'm throwing your others away. I'm tired of your waking me up to help you match your shirts and trousers. Now they'll always match."

"That's a lot of white," Wayman remembered saying.

Still standing, he lifted his right foot and tugged on a sock. He recognized this one-leg-balancing business as a kind of genetic pride. Right into his seventies, Wayman's father had been in the habit of jumping up in the living room in front of guests—the more the better—doubling one stocky leg up under him, touching his knee to the floor, straightening up, and repeating the process, saying, "How about this? Call *me* an old codger, will they?" Wayman thought he might have been able to duplicate his father's feat about the time he graduated from high school, when he was a miler on the track team, but he wasn't sure. His legs were long and skinny, and it was farther to the floor. He compromised by putting on his shoes and socks this way every morning.

"Wayman's flamingo act," Willa had said once, out on the deck. At least a dozen people had been there, all from Heartland Cad-Geo: Bill Shipley and his wife, Jerry Beltz and his wife then, Joel Messenger, the parts manager, Jeff Northcutt, Sally—Sally Leith then, before she changed back to her maiden name, Frazer; she and Willa had been in high school together—and some others. Wayman had been salesman of the month three times straight, so he owed them a party. He had baked a big pot of beans and grilled steaks, and Willa had made potato salad and margaritas. That had stopped when Willa went to school. While Willa was describing how he did it—pull the sock and then the shoe on his right foot, set his right foot down, put on the left sock and shoe, set his left foot down, lift his right foot back up, tie the shoelace, then the left—and he was laughing with the others, he had glanced over to find Sally's eyes on him. She wasn't even smiling. He had squirmed, looked away, got up to bring the jug of margaritas. How had Willa gotten on the subject? Bantering with Jerry about something. She had a way then, when she was having a good time, of gazing off to a man's left and all of a sudden whipping her head to his right, showing one profile and then the other. Her brown hair lifting and falling, her mouth a perfect bow, lipsticked in those days. Sally's expression puzzled Wayman; it reminded him of someone who had opened the wrong door at the wrong time.

Wayman looked regretfully at the drawn blind. If Willa were up he could open it, let the light in. He tied his right shoelace, then his left. Another day: am I ready? Yes. Rested and ready. Willa sighed loudly again, a sort of huffing sound, and turned back to her right side, jerking the sheet over her head.

In the kitchen, Elizabeth had finished her yogurt-banana-orange juice smoothie and was ready to go. "Does Sally Frazer still work at Heartland?" she asked.

"Sure," Wayman said. "Why?"

"I saw her in a booth at the mall yesterday, selling her birdhouses."

"In a booth?" He stared at Elizabeth. "Nah."

"Yah," she mimicked him. "But I don't think she was doing very well. Mom in bed?"

Wayman nodded. "Still asleep." His daughter had two extra earrings in one ear, blue stones not much bigger than pinheads. Nothing in her nose or eyebrows, or elsewhere, as far as Wayman knew. No tattoos, also as far as he knew, though she had talked about getting one last year. Some of her friends, the ones with car stereos that rattled the dishes in the dining-room hutch, had things like sea horses and leering skulls on their arms and legs. In junior high she had contacts and belonged to a pep club, but now she wore glasses with black wire rims. Her hair, darker than her mother's used to be, was braided back neatly in what Wayman had learned not to call a pigtail. Sometimes, when he watched her coming out of school after her physics or Spanish club meetings, he thought of those commercials where a prim young woman stepped into a red convertible, shook out her hair, and flung her glasses and briefcase into the backseat.

Elizabeth rattled the spoon loudly in her rinsed glass. "No wonder she's sleeping. She was still out at midnight."

"What were you doing up?"

"Homework. If I can do mine here, why can't she?"

"Honey, she's in a university. The library's open all night there."

"Hey." Elizabeth waggled a grey book from her backpack under his nose. "I was doing trig. She's taking the same basic math she dropped last spring."

As he drove the Accord down Fremont Avenue toward her school, Elizabeth twisted inside her safety belt without unbuckling it and squared her shoulders against the door. Wayman had learned to recognize this danger signal. "So," she said, "doesn't it bother you that Mom comes in late every night?"

"Not every night. No, it doesn't." He resisted what seemed like a sensible urge to put up his forearms, like a boxer protecting himself.

"How's your sex life?" Elizabeth asked.

He leveled his finger at her as he felt his ears redden. "*That*—"

"Is none of my business." She smirked. "But you answered my question anyway."

"I did not."

She leaned forward against her shoulder belt. "Actually, it *is* my business, in a way. Do you understand what I mean?"

"No, I don't, and I don't know how kids—you—can even think of saying things to their parents like that." Wayman swung into the block-long circle drive at the high school, found a space at the curb, and stopped. "What the hell are they teaching you at this place, anyway?"

Elizabeth regarded him for a long moment before she unbuckled her seat belt. When she answered, Wayman heard a hint of the little-girl plaintiveness she used to have in her voice. Ten years ago, maybe. "Don't worry about what they're teaching us here, Dad. That's not the problem."

What was it Willa used to say—"If there's one thing I can't

stand, it's a precocious child"? Watching his daughter stride toward the building, Wayman felt like leaning out the window and yelling, "It's all right, Sweetheart! It's okay!" Someone behind him honked, wanting the curb space. Now he would worry all day long.

But as he drove to Heartland he noted the russet on the pin oaks and the sunlight glinting warmly off the yellowing, heart-shaped leaves of the redbud trees, and his spirits rose. Sally at the mall, with a booth: good for her. The birdhouse she'd given him, blushing—she blushed a lot—looked exactly like a brick cottage, complete with chimney and curtains at the windows. Like real bricks. A pair of Carolina wrens had lived in it four or five years now. The bulldozers on the site of the new Sycamores Mall, which would quadruple the traffic past Heartland, were sparing not only the tallest sycamores but the white oaks too, and even a few hills, Wayman noted; the developer appeared to have a soul. Wayman had read that the outside shops would have broad sidewalks, benches, shade trees, plots of flowers. There was a "now leasing" sign by each of the entrances.

His spirits climbed another notch when, minutes after the showroom doors were unlocked, Ginger Cochran of the banker Cochrans arrived, a full year early, to trade in her DeVille.

"What's wrong with it?" Wayman asked her. "I thought you liked it."

Ginger laughed. Her country-club-tennis tan gave her crinkles around the eyes that made her look sixty, which Wayman knew she was, but she moved and talked more like thirty. "Nothing's wrong with it. Mother and I are taking a cruise to Alaska. We thought it'd be fun to drive to Seattle, and then we thought, what the heck—we might as well do it in a new car."

"Alaska? Isn't it already winter up there?"

"Now, we've decided, so don't try to talk me out of it, either the trip or the car," Ginger said. "Why do I have to twist your arm to make you sell me a car?"

This was a perennial mock-complaint of Ginger's, much embellished and not strictly true. Years ago, when he was still the new guy, Wayman had talked her out of a commission-padding mahogany dash panel, to the disgust of Bill Shipley, the sales manager. Six months later a similar dash on Ginger's detested real-estate-tycoon neighbor's car had warped back like the horns on a water buffalo, and Ginger had literally hugged Wayman in glee when she told him. The incident and its aftermath had established him as Ginger's man at Heartland, and, gradually, the salesman other Cochrans came to as well. He was known, he heard now and then, as an honest car salesman; even Willa had told him so. That reputation, he had once assumed, would make him the sales manager when Bill Shipley retired, but the job went to Jerry Beltz instead, who later told Wayman that he'd been passed over partly because of the Cochrans. "Bill nursed a little grudge about you and them—they were his, till you came along. The other thing's about you being so honest. The Heartland people weren't sure that's what they needed in a sales manager."

When Wayman told Willa, he said he supposed, weird as it sounded, that he should feel good about missing the promotion. As she snatched a twenty-dollar bill from his hand to pay the Pizza Hut delivery boy, she had answered, "If selling cars is what you do for a living, then why not be a car salesman?"

While Sally was doing the paperwork on Ginger's calypso green DeVille—her trade-in was dark cherry—Jeff Northcutt palmed off a bent, shuffling octogenarian on Wayman.

"Sorry to do it," Jeff muttered as he headed toward a woman in a silvery fur who was peering into an El Dorado Touring Coupe, "but that ain't no coonskin she's got on."

The old fellow wanted the red, five-speed, two-door Prizm parked outside the showroom, and had the cash to buy it. Wayman had scarcely seen Ginger out the door, simultaneously shepherding the elderly man to Sally's desk, when he found himself in the midst of a deal for a Tracker with a young couple wearing khaki hiking outfits. An hour later Sally was buried under so much paper she had stopped making jokes or even complaining about the work he'd stacked on her, and he was selling a Seville ST to a cousin of Ginger Cochran's and, by cellular telephone, a Metro to the cousin's daughter, who was a student at Drury College. Out of the corner of his eye he noted Jerry Beltz at his office door, looking stunned.

Then, momentarily, he too was stunned.

"Like, what's the, like, you know," the daughter said, when an idea blindsided him: a suspicion, disturbingly strong, that something very strange had happened at home that morning. What? It was real, he was sure, but exactly what it was eluded him. He couldn't put his finger on it, and anyway, didn't want to.

"Sorry, Miss," he said. "It's noisy here. You were saying."

"Like, I'm concerned about the depletion of fossil—you know?" the Cochran cousin's daughter said. "So, like, the Metro—"

"Like, still the best mileage," Wayman said. "Until they figure out how to burn water, you can't do better."

He was moving fast. He sold another car. And another.

At half-past two he remembered he hadn't eaten lunch, but a long-time customer caught him as he started toward the sandwich vending machine, and he forgot again. He sold two more cars after that.

"Busier 'n a snowcone stand in hell," he said to Sally as he slid yet another set of papers under those beside her computer.

She regarded him soberly, a little like that time at the party, before she smiled. "Best you've ever done, Wayman. Congratulations."

"Thanks. Hey, Elizabeth said you were selling your birdhouses at the mall."

She tapped her space bar loudly, a blush spreading over her squarish face. Her dark hair, cut and flipped in a neat way that was probably old-fashioned now, would be salt-and-peppery in a few more years. "Saturday and Sunday," she said. "I didn't break even. They charge a lot for those booths."

"You gave it a shot," Wayman said. "Good for you."

She smiled again. "It was fun. I wish I could sell the way you can. What a day you've had."

It was true. He'd never had such a day. Only as he went to pick up Elizabeth did he find the time to be amazed, not so much at the money he had made but at how well he had juggled customers and sales talk and numbers—and yes, Sally too—had moved from Ginger Cochran to the old man, to the hikers to Jerry's office, back to the hikers (they had balked over the trade-in for half an hour), to Jerry's office, to Sally, to the Cochran cousin and his daughter. Efficiently, purposefully: he'd been here, there, exactly when he should have been. Kept all the balls in the air. The other salesmen had not sold a car, so far as he knew. He felt bad about that, but not guilty; he had not intentionally or even unintentionally elbowed anyone aside to get to a customer. Some of it was luck, of course. The expensively dressed woman that Jeff Northcutt shucked the old man for had strolled out five minutes later, saying she was just curious; she never bought anything but Lincoln Town Cars.

Wayman turned onto Fremont Avenue. In the air; kept all the—

"Hunh!" He hit the brake hard. A van swerved and honked as it passed him.

The disturbing but vague notion that had glanced off earlier returned, but this time it smacked him head on. "Hunh!" he said a second time, and, frowning, pulled over and stopped half a block short of the circle drive at the high school. That morning as he had dressed—no, it was when he was putting on his shoes and socks. Tying his shoes. He resisted even as the idea metamorphosed from wavering outline to a cast-iron fact, but he could not overcome his conviction that it had happened. He had been thinking; what about? White shirts, his father. Sally, Willa. The hummingbird. But out at the edge of his mind he had watched himself as, after he had put the sock and then the shoe on his right foot, he had taken the other sock from the bed, drawn his left leg up, and repeated the process. He remembered that Willa had huffed and flopped over as he tied the laces. But he also remembered something else: *He had not put his right foot back down on the floor.* He had hung there. Hovered there.

"Idiot," he said sternly, and reached for the gearshift. He turned off the engine instead.

That peripheral video camera in his mind had kept on recording, it seemed to Wayman; now he saw himself, after he had tied the second shoe, look at the window blind and wish it were raised, turn to the dresser, slip his wallet into his hip pocket and his fountain pen into his shirt pocket, and pick up his keys and his brown jacket. Then, and only then, he had finally put both feet on the floor at the same time and walked down the hall toward the kitchen.

"Dad!" Elizabeth rapped on the window, not, Wayman realized, for the first time. "Are you all right? Why'd you stop here?"

He unlocked her door. "Sorry. My mind was a million miles—"

"No kidding," she said. "What's going on?"

"Nothing," he answered. "Hey, how was your day?"

"Never mind mine. It's yours we better talk about."

"I had a great day." Seeing her disbelief, Wayman smiled. "I mean it. I've just had one of the best days of my life." His widening smile felt good, even though his face seemed to be audibly cracking. How long had it been since he'd smiled like that?

"So why'd you stop here?" she asked.

He winked at her as he swung the car into traffic. "All of a sudden I had this idea I was a hummingbird."

"Sure you did." The corners of her mouth curled in disgust, then straightened before she asked, "Were you worried about what I said this morning?"

"No."

"You sure?"

"Yep." Without looking, he knew she was shifting around in the seat again, but he felt no urge to throw up his arms for protection. *If a man can hover like that, why should he worry*; he suppressed a smirk. "So what were you saying? You think your mother might be involved with some other man?"

He felt a little surge of triumph as she hesitated. Just say it right out, he thought. Bluff and blunt; that's the ticket.

"Why does it have to be a man?" she asked.

"Hunh!" he said once more. Something inside—his whole skeleton, it seemed like—sagged, and he felt as plaintive as the tone he'd heard in Elizabeth's voice that morning.

His daughter began, "Don't be mad—"

"I'm not mad," he said. "But how do you ... where do you come up with such ideas? Does she tell you things like that? I can't imagine it."

Elizabeth shook her head. "We don't talk much. But I go on the campus too, and I've seen her with people. And at Corey's."

Corey's was one of those coffee places. Willa had told him that, and also that Elizabeth went there. Neither of them drank coffee at home. "With someone in particular?" he asked. "Is that what you're saying?"

"Yes." As Elizabeth turned toward the windshield, he noticed a reddish glint above the two blue stones in her ear. "I'm not trying to be a pain in the ass, Dad. I'm telling you she's changing. She *has* changed. You're just drifting along, but she's not."

"What's that thing on your ear? When'd you get that?"

"*Dad*. This is serious."

"She's going to leave me? Us?"

"Maybe. Probably." He felt Elizabeth look at him. "Could you take that?"

Shoulders squared up and jaw rigid, he said, "Leave me for a woman?" When was the last time he had braced himself like that? Eating an artichoke heart. In an Italian restaurant, in some olive-oily concoction Willa had gotten him to try. It hadn't been so bad.

They were silent in the heavy traffic on Sunshine Street, but as he turned into their subdivision, Wayman said, "What do you mean, 'drifting'? I sell cars. I work five, six days a week. Sometimes seven. I pay your mother's school expenses. She bought $300 worth of books this semester. I pay your expenses. Is that drifting?"

"I worked at TCBY last summer," Elizabeth reminded him.

He nodded. "You bought your own clothes. But still—is that drifting?"

"You've been doing it a long time, Dad. Since before I was born."

"Is it a crime to stay with a job you're good at? Pretty good at most of the time?"

"But can't you just about sell cars in your sleep?"

"It's not that simple," Wayman said. "You have to keep up with all the models. Cylinders. Airbags. Turning radiuses. Some people will walk off if you can't tell them on the spot how much of a Prizm is American made. Most don't give a hoot, but you have to be ready." Remembering the simultaneous sales to Ginger Cochran's cousin and his daughter, Wayman thought, I can just about do it. Some days I can almost sell them in my sleep.

"Surprise. The fire truck's here." Elizabeth jerked her thumb at Willa's Geo as they stopped in the carport, then turned to Wayman. "Okay, you have to know all those things, but still," she thumped the dash of the Accord before she picked up her backpack, "you don't even drive what you sell. Do you know *this* car's turning radius?"

Wayman grinned. "You got me there."

He tugged off his tie as he went down the hallway, wondering where Willa was, and found her sitting on the edge of the bed.

"I saw you this morning," she said as he hung up his tie and jacket in the closet. He was aware of her watching him. She was wearing a light blue sweater patterned with scattering white leaves that he had always liked.

"You did? At Heartland?"

"No. Right there." She pointed at the end of the bed.

The *whump* in his chest reminded him of those car speakers Elizabeth's friends had. He said, "What do you mean, saw me?"

Willa closed the door and locked it. He had not noticed that her sweater was unbuttoned. She looked to his left, then his right. "I think you know exactly what I mean," she said.

Twenty minutes later, she moved slightly away from his now-sweaty side, then snuggled her head into the hollow of his shoulder. "Wow." She was still breathing hard. "Like amorous birds of prey, huh?"

Her short hair itched, so he nudged her to a more comfortable spot. "Birds of prey what?" he said.

"'Amorous birds of prey.' Like eagles doing it in mid-air. The idea of that predatoriness rechanneled as sexual—"

"I get it," Wayman said. *Mid-air*, he thought. So she had seen him; it wasn't a nutty half-dream he'd recalled. He wondered if she would go on to explain how he had done it, but he wasn't curious about it; he wasn't even surprised that he didn't care. He thought about Elizabeth's suspicion, or accusation; should he say something now? Without dragging their daughter into it, of course. *Willa, is there anything you need to tell me?* Something like that. Then what?

"Going back to the campus tonight?" he asked.

"Maybe," Willa said. "I've got a report due that I could write here, but I also need to look up some stuff at the library. Oh, by the way, I've applied for some assistantships for graduate school." She got up and began to dress.

Wayman got up too. He said, "I guess you don't mean just here. At this school."

"Well, it doesn't make much sense to limit myself that way."

"To limit your chances," he said.

Willa nodded. "Right."

He gestured at the rumpled bed. "So was this a ... a sort of ..."

"Valedictory?" she asked.

"Yes, if that means what it sounds like."

She pulled up her jeans and buttoned them, then studied him for a moment. "I don't know if we need to be so dramatic, or terminal. You seem to be well prepared, in any case."

After dinner—spaghetti Willa made with canned sauce and Polish sausage, and a salad that Elizabeth tossed with tomatoes he brought in from their garden—Wayman changed the syrup in the hummingbird feeder. Two or three weeks, four at the most, and the little guy would head south. The wrens stay, the cardinals too, but the hummingbirds go, Wayman thought; we do what we have to. What we can. He turned the Bears-Vikings Monday-night game on, then off without learning the score. Elizabeth was studying at the kitchen table. He picked up the telephone just as Willa came into the living room, now wearing over her jeans a green sweatshirt decorated with a picture of what appeared to be a heavily bejeweled egg. Wayman hung up.

"Who are you calling?" she asked.

"Sally."

She rummaged in the outside pocket of her backpack, then

pulled out her car keys.

"What about?"

He shrugged. "Birds, I guess."

"That makes sense," she said, and after she and Elizabeth exchanged goodbyes and the back door closed, he heard the Geo start and leave.

"I'm so mad I could spit," Sally said. "Do you know what that asshole Jerry Beltz told me as I was leaving today? That he doesn't approve—*approve*, mind you—of me peddling my birdhouses in the mall."

Wayman listened as Sally reeled off Jerry's mental and moral failings. When she paused for breath, he asked, "So did you quit?"

"Well, no. But I wanted to."

"I've been thinking about your birdhouses. And how you know so much about birds. And birdseed," Wayman said. "Have you noticed all the big trees they're leaving at that Sycamores Mall?"

"I did notice," Sally said. "Why?"

Elizabeth appeared at the kitchen door, her glasses tilted down over her nose. Wayman thought the mixture of anticipation, uncertainty, and, yes, fear on her face about matched his own.

"Hovering," he said to Sally. "I've been sort of hovering over an idea."

Susan Perabo

*I know I risk not being taken seriously as a writer by
admitting what I'm about to admit, but I'd like to have it on
the record anyway: My early childhood was nothing short of
a thrill ride, so jam packed with excitement and joy that I
could often hardly contain myself. That's my big sister Betsy
on the right; she probably did most of the real work on this
snowman while I ran around our front yard, screaming,
flailing my arms, simply beside myself with happiness.*

Susan Perabo is the writer-in-residence at Dickinson College in Carlisle,
Pennsylvania. She holds an MFA from the University of Arkansas,
Fayetteville. Her work has appeared in *Best American Short Stories, New
Stories from the South, Story, TriQuarterly*, the *Black Warrior Review*, and other
publications. Her first collection of short stories, *Who I Was Supposed to Be*,
was published by Simon & Schuster this past fall.

SUSAN PERABO
The Greater Grace of Carlisle

*M*y mother, beside herself with loss, spent $35,000 on lottery tickets in nine months. It was Mr. Jenkins from next door, the official neighborhood bearer of bad news, who finally called to tell me.

"You know I don't like to tattle …," he began. He ended with: "We thought you should know."

I thanked him. I had thanked him as a teenager when he peeled my cat off the road and brought her limp body to our front door. Funny, the things you wind up thanking people for.

My stepfather Walt had died the previous January, after almost two years of battling stomach cancer. Through it all, my mother was the poster child for well-adjusted spouses of the terminally ill. For twenty-one months, her good will and sound judgment bordered on the psychotic. And after he died—after he finally, finally died—she seemed fine. Well, not exactly fine, but up to speed for a grieving widow. She wept as she packed away his flannel shirts, even had a session of grief therapy with the minister at their Methodist church. And then she seemed to go on with her life. I stayed with her for two weeks and then returned to my own crumbling world, a thousand miles away. As I bitched my way through a separation and second divorce in Arizona, my mother was going crazy in Illinois, trying desperately to win the lottery.

"We've discussed it," Mr. Jenkins said. I didn't ask who the "we" was, probably him and his tropical fish. "We think you should probably come for a visit."

At the time, I was doing temp work in Phoenix. I was also doing temp life. I had moved there only a year before with my ex-husband; what friends I had made were the wives and girlfriends of the men at his office, women I had not had time to bond with profoundly enough to warrant the inevitable awkwardness of post-divorce friendship. I had suffered through this period before, with another husband in another state, so I knew what to expect: the occasional pity call, an offer for a lunch date that never materialized, empty well wishing that was worse than no wishing at all.

"I'll be there," I told Mr. Jenkins.

And so I returned to my childhood home of Carlisle, Illinois, population thirty-five hundred morons. My mother didn't admit anything for two days. I was afraid to spring it on her, wary of pointing fingers at my mother, who (like the good fourth-grade teacher she had been for thirty-two years) always told me that when you point a finger at somebody you've got three fingers pointing back at yourself. I didn't want any more fingers pointed at me for the rest of my life, so I tried the subtle approach.

Day one:
  "Where's your car?"
  "I didn't need it any longer. I sold it."
  "Don't you ever drive anywhere?"
  "I can walk to the market, you know. I'm not feeble."

Night one:
"You still have that stock?"
"The market is shaky. Besides, that was Walt's game."

Day two:
"Where's Grandma's silver?"
"I don't know. Somewhere in the attic."
"I sure love that silver."
"Really? I always thought it was ugly."

Night two:
"You still have that teacher's pension coming, don't you?"
She put down her glass of wine. "Chatty Chatty Kathy," she said, raising her eyebrows. "I'm beginning to think you have an ulterior motive."
"I just want to make sure you're financially sound," I said. "Don't you read magazines? All these eighty-five year olds end up working the drive-thru window at McDonald's because they've squandered their money."
"I won't be working at McDonald's," she said.
"I was just—"
"It's sad," she said. "I thought we were fairly close. I'd expect this type of sneaky behavior from your brothers, but not you. Next thing you'll be following me to the market."
"Why would I want to follow you to the market?"
She smiled slyly. "What time is it?"
I looked at my watch.
"Don't tell me," she said. She closed her eyes and held up her left hand as if testing the breeze in the dining room. "It's 6:45, isn't it?"
I was impressed. "How'd you know?"
"I've developed a sixth sense. You know what happens in twelve minutes?"
"What?"

She rose from her chair. "We get rich."

She dropped her napkin on the table and drifted off into the living room. A moment later I joined her. She was sitting cross-legged on the floor in front of the television, a six-inch stack of lottery tickets in front of her.

"How many?" I asked.

"Hm?" she said. "Three hundred."

I sunk down on the couch. "You spend three hundred dollars a day on lottery tickets?"

"Don't be stupid. They only draw three times a week."

"Nine hundred dollars a week."

"Nine hundred dollars will be like nine cents in about five minutes."

I sat back and crossed my legs. Following a brief trumpet fanfare, the lottery man came on the TV, wearing a suit and tie and a hairpiece of questionable quality. A scantily clad Illinois farm girl with hair down to her butt was pulling ping-pong balls out of a chute. The numbers were announced. My mother scribbled them down on a sheet of paper, then began going through her tickets.

"Gimme half," I said. "I'll help."

"Not a chance," she said.

So I sat there and watched her go through her tickets. It took twenty minutes. She scanned each one and set it off to her right, beside her on the floor. She didn't speak, made no noises of defeat. When she had scanned the last ticket (twice, I noticed) she picked up the pile and stood up and left me sitting there on the couch. I followed her into the kitchen. She threw the tickets away and started washing the dishes.

"Well?" I said.

"Well what?"

"You didn't win."

She turned off the water, turned to me. "No," she said. "I just didn't win *today*. On Wednesday I'll have three hundred more chances."

"I don't think this is very healthy," I said.

"Neither is smoking," she said.

"I don't smoke."

"I didn't say that you did. But millions of people do. And millions of people drive their cars too fast and millions of people clog their veins with cholesterol and none of those people are healthy either."

"Mother…," I said.

"Don't you 'Mother' me."

"How much money do you have left?"

"Enough."

I laughed. "Enough for what?"

She turned back to the dishes. "Enough to buy you a plane ticket back to Phoenix."

The next morning when I went out for the mail, Mr. Jenkins was next door mowing his lawn on his riding mower. His lawn is no larger than your average suburban lawn, but he had owned this riding mower for as long as I could remember and mowed his lawn at least twice a week. While I stood at the mailbox he waved me over and cut the engine. He wiped sweat from his brow, although it was cool out, September, and I wondered how somebody could get sweaty riding around on a little tractor.

"How's Hildy?" he asked. "You get her to stop buying those tickets?"

"Not yet," I said.

He took my arm. "You know whatcha do?" he said. "Across town, there's this church. They got anonymous groups there for everything, got people all over this area coming in to get fixed. They got your standard Triple A, then they got anonymous shoppers, anonymous dopers, anonymous homosexuals, anonymous spouses." He leaned into me. "They even got that anonymous necrophiliacs."

"Nymphomaniacs?" I ventured.

"The sex junkies," he said. "Whatever you call them. And they got one for gamblers, like Hildy. You should take her down there, Kathy, see if they can set her straight."

"I'm not sure that's necessary," I said.

He shrugged. "She's your family." He reached to start the mower, but then stopped. "Heard you got divorced again," he said. He landed on the "again" like he had run over a dog with his lawnmower.

"Yes," I said.

"You're a good girl, Kathy," he said. "Why don't the boys see that?"

"I don't know, Mr. Jenkins," I said.

In junior high school my best friend Melinda Marietta used to say: "You can't get your period in Carlisle without half the town knowing about it." Pretty close to the truth. Out for my daily walk that afternoon, I felt the eyes of the people on our block settle on me from porches and bay windows, and I imagined they all knew that my mother was spending her teacher's pension (more importantly *their* tax dollars, after all) on lottery tickets. I ignored them as best I could, walked down the ragged sidewalks, past the old post office, and found myself on Locust Street. Before I knew it—yes, idiot Mr. Jenkins had gotten to me—I was standing in front of a fading brick building, one of two hundred just like it in the historic district, with a white sign on the front that said *The Greater Grace of Carlisle*. It didn't really look like a church, although the glass doors were propped open and I could hear what sounded like a choir singing from the basement. I took a few steps in and looked around. There was an office, and the door was open, so I peeked in and saw a heavy man in jeans and a turtleneck sweater sitting at a desk reading a magazine.

"Hello?" I said.

He looked up from his magazine, smiled. "What can I do for you?"

"I heard you have groups here," I said. "I was looking for something for a friend, something about gambling?"

He motioned me to a chair. I sat down and he folded his hands on the desk in front of him. "First," he said. "Let me tell you. We are all gamblers, and we are all anonymous. There's no need to be ashamed."

"It's not me," I said. "It's my mother."

"Ah hah?" he said, intrigued. "Your mother … I see. What's her addiction?"

"She buys lottery tickets."

He slammed his fist down on the desk. "Goddamn lottery," he shouted. "Goddamn helps-the-schools, helps-the-elderly, helps-the-highways lottery."

"This a common problem?"

He breathed a heavy sigh. "Problem, no. Epidemic, yes," he said. "Does your mother know you're here?"

"God, no," I said. "She doesn't think she has a problem. Or an epidemic."

"They never do," he said wistfully. He stared off over my head for a moment, frowning at the concept of addiction as if it were hovering in the doorway. "You'll have to get her to come to group," he finally said. "We meet every Wednesday, in the basement." He smiled at the voices rising from the floor. "That's our choir."

"It's not singers anonymous?"

He didn't smile. "Wednesday," he said. "Tomorrow night, seven o'clock. It's an intimate group. You may come if you wish, the first time, if necessary."

"You mean if I have to drag her?"

"We don't drag," he said sincerely. "We nudge."

"Who runs the group?"

"I do," he said. He extended his hand across the desk. "I'm Brother James."

I didn't ask whose brother he was. I had enough brothers, four of them, all in their forties and far away with wives and kids whose names I usually couldn't remember. To them, all of them, Carlisle, Illinois was like a disease; it had infected my mother and they were damned if it was going to get them too. I understood how they felt. The most famous people from our town were Eddie Wills, who got a football scholarship to the University of Illinois, sat on the Fighting Illini bench for four years, and returned to open a shoe store downtown, and Bud Porter, who stepped on a land mine in Vietnam and for twenty-five years had sat everyday at the table at the Sheetz drinking cherry Slurpees and letting kids touch his fiberglass leg. The sign when you entered Carlisle read: *Home of the 3A Cross-Country District Champs, 1984—Go Bees!*

My mother was in her vegetable garden. It's small, but prosperous, supplying most of the neighborhood with tomatoes and green peppers for the majority of the summer. She was wearing jeans and a White Sox sweatshirt, some ragged gardening gloves with faded strawberries, and a big splintering straw hat. This was the kind of image that humiliated me as a child. Now, standing at the kitchen window, I found it comforting.

"Turn on the hose!" she shouted at me.

I went out back and turned the rusty knob, then joined her beside her tomato plants, which were withering, already preparing themselves for the first frost, their timely deaths.

"Long walk," she said.

I sat down on the soft earth beside her, twisted some grass around my finger.

"Did you go down to the park?" she asked. "Those ducks are—"

"You've got a problem," I said.

She adjusted her hat. "Just one?"

"Ha ha."

"All right, what's my problem?"

"You're going to be broke in a year. You're going to lose this house, Mother."

"Not if I win."

"You're not going to win," I said. "You are never going to win."

She set down her spade, brushed some hair from her forehead with the back of her hand. "What makes you so sure?"

"I'm just sure."

"That's a lousy answer. I wouldn't accept that from fourth graders, so I'm certainly not going to accept it from you."

"Okay, then," I said. "What makes you so sure you will win?"

"God told me."

This gave me pause. Then I thought: this is my mother; things can only get so weird. "Tell me you're kidding," I said.

"Of course I'm kidding. What kind of lunatic do you think I am?"

"Listen," I said. "There's this church down on Locust, this—"

"I know all about it," she interrupted. "Mr. Jenkins keeps leaving their literature in my mailbox. I see him sneaking out there after he thinks I've gone to bed."

"Go for me," I said. "Just one time, just tomorrow night. Go for me."

"I can't tomorrow. There's a drawing."

"So you can tape it and watch it when we get home," I said. "Look at it this way—you can live in blissful denial for an extra two hours."

She smiled wistfully, and a gust of wind knocked her hat to the ground.

When Brother James said the group was intimate, he wasn't kidding. There were only three people there when we arrived, besides the Brother. My mother took one look at them sitting around the little conference table in the basement and turned back towards the stairs. I blocked her exit and she entered the room with a flourish, as if she were entering a cocktail party.

"Hello, all," she said cheerily.

"Come in, come in," Brother James said, waving us to join.

The members of the group introduced themselves. Rick, definitely a corn farmer, was there with his tense wife. It was his first time too. Then there was a tall and lanky guy, Andy. He was unshaven and wore a ripped army jacket, looked like he had made a wrong turn on the way to the homeless shelter.

Farmer Rick, it turned out, had a card problem. He had played a friendly game of poker with some friends once a week for twenty years, so friendly, in fact, that he had lost all of his wife's savings to his friends.

"And Andy?" Brother James said.

"I'm your run-of-the-mill equestrian addict," Andy said.

"Forgive me," the farmer's wife said, her cheeks reddening. "We're new at this. Is that like LSD?"

Brother James sighed. "Andy bets money on horses," he said. "And Hildegard?"

"Hildy, please," my mother said, flushing.

"Hildy?"

"I enjoy buying a few lottery tickets," she said.

I snorted, and she shot me a look.

"What's a few?" Brother James asked.

I opened my mouth but he raised a hand to shush me.

"Three hundred each drawing," my mother said. "But I have plenty of money, I can afford it. And I'm not addicted."

"See?" Farmer Rick said to his wife. "See? What'd I tell you?"

My mother, sensing an ally, turned to him and smiled. "You're not addicted either?"

"Oh, that's not what I meant," he said. "No, I was just telling her earlier that it could be worse, that I could be buying lottery tickets."

My mother paused. Then she said: "This from a poker player."

"Well now," Brother James said, grasping his hands together. "Looks like it's time for our first lesson. We work as a team. A team. We're here to support each other, not cut each other down."

"But it's much more interesting that way, Brother James," Andy piped in.

Brother James grimaced. "Andy's been with us for quite a while," he said. "He's seen a lot of people cured, haven't you Andy?"

Andy shrugged. "Sure. Then most of them start turning up on Mondays."

"What's Mondays?" the farmer's wife asked hopefully.

"AA," Andy said.

Brother James forced a chuckle. Andy smiled. He had incredibly straight teeth. He caught me looking at him and winked in my direction. My mother sighed.

After the group was over, Andy cornered me outside the door. "I'm heading over to the track," he said. "You want to come?"

"No thanks," I said. "What track?"

"Kathy...," my mother said. "We need to get home."

"Fairmount Park," Andy said. He stretched his long arms over his head, yawned.

"That's three hours from here," I said.

"My lucky track this month," he said. "Wanna come? Great nachos."

"I hate nachos," I said.

He shrugged. "Suit yourself, daughter of lottery addict."
"I'm not an addict," my mother said.

This time, I refused to watch the drawing with her. I sat on
my old bed in my old room flipping through an old *People
Magazine*. Princess Diana was on the cover, smiling with baby
William, having no idea she would end up bulimic and
divorced and dead.

My mother appeared in the doorway, holding a single ticket
in the air.

"What?" I asked. I had an instant—a tiny and surprisingly beautiful moment—where I believed that she had actually won.

"Four numbers," she said. "*Four* numbers. I'm getting closer, Kathy."

I threw the magazine on my lap. "You're not getting closer. Luck is not something you can get *closer* at. Did I dream it, or were you not once a teacher, a fairly sensible person?"

"How can you sit with those people for two hours and come away thinking I have a problem? They're obviously far worse off than I am."

"Mother, addiction is not measured by degrees."

"Oh my God," she said. "You're becoming one of them. You left your life in Phoenix for this?"

Then, sitting there in my old bed in my old room with my old mother, I felt myself start to crack. It crept in my toes and up my thighs and through my stomach and past my heart and into my head and—much to my humiliation—I felt my eyes well up with tears. It wasn't that I had left anything behind in Phoenix that got to me; it was that I *hadn't* left anything behind in Phoenix. You should not be thirty-five years old and be able to leave your home behind with a day's notice. There should be people to call, troubles to iron out, explanations to give. But there had been none of that. I didn't even get a newspaper.

"Oh, honey," my mother said, coming to my bed. "I didn't mean it. You're nothing like them, really."

"I can't believe I'm back in this town," I said. "I can't believe I'm back in this shitty town and it's exactly the same as when I left and *I'm* exactly the same as when I left."

"No you're not," she said, petting my cheek. "You're all grown up."

I swatted her hand away. "What exactly has changed? I'm a two-time loser, Mother. Just ask Mr. Jenkins or anybody else in the neighborhood."

"I'm a two-time loser, too," she said.

"Yeah, but one of your husbands died, so it doesn't really count. You're like a two-time loser with an asterisk. You didn't *blow it* twice."

"Maybe I did," she said. "How do you know? Maybe I was blowing it with Walt and he died before we could go through with the divorce."

I wiped my nose, amazed. "Is that true?"

"Well, no," she said. "But it could be. All I'm saying is there are always circumstances, honey. It's never as simple as it sounds. Who cares what people think?"

"You don't care that people think you're crazy?"

"I care that my daughter thinks I'm crazy. That's why I went tonight. But no, it makes no difference to me what other people think."

"Then you're crazy," I said.

"Maybe so," she said. She stood up, waved the nearly successful lottery ticket above my bed. "But when I'm rich everyone will say I'm merely eccentric."

The next day I was lying on the couch watching TV when my mother stuck her head into the living room. "I don't mean to alarm you," she said. "But your boyfriend's been sitting in the front yard for ten minutes."

"Funny," I said, not raising my head from the pillow.

"I'm not kidding." She opened the blinds, and I sat up to see out the window. Andy, the pony better, was sitting beside the mailbox. When he saw us looking at him he waved.

"What's he doing here?"

"I couldn't imagine."

"Maybe he's here for you, you know, for a little impromptu group therapy."

"I sincerely doubt that," she said. "Now go on out and tell

him to stop lazing in the front yard before Mr. Jenkins calls the police."

I got up and went warily to the door, opened it, and stepped out onto the porch.

"Hi there," he called. "Want to go for a stroll?"

"A what?"

"You know," he said, standing. "A stroll. Like walking, but happier."

Well, I decided, I hadn't had my walk today. And I did need to get him off the yard. I closed the front door and joined him on the lawn and he started walking.

"What're you up to today?" he asked.

"Nothing," I said. "TV."

"Sounds fun," he said. I couldn't tell if he was being sarcastic or not, so I didn't respond.

"You're from around here, aren't you?" Andy asked.

"How'd you guess? The tattoo on my forehead?"

"I remember you," he said. "You were a couple years ahead of me in high school. When'd you graduate? 'Eighty-two? 'Eighty-three?"

"Something like that," I said.

"You played the cello, right?"

"I supported the cello," I said. "And I moved the bow. I wouldn't go so far as to say I played it."

He grinned. We turned the corner onto Spruce Street, heading towards the Sheetz. "Check this out," he said. He reached into his pocket and pulled out a wad of bills. "Ninety bucks," he said. "Down to five measly dollars and I nailed the last race. There's some grace for you, huh? Can I buy you a Slurpee?"

We were now standing in front of the Sheetz. School had let out, and there were several little Bees buzzing around, smoking cigarettes and flirting. We went into the store. Bud Porter was sitting with his leg propped up in the booth, slurping his Slurpee and reading *Mad Magazine.*

"Hey, Budster," Andy said.

"Hey, Andster," Bud Porter said.

I let Andy buy me a grape Slurpee and we went and sat down in the booth behind Bud Porter.

"Blowing off work for a date, Andy?" Bud asked, not looking up from his magazine.

"I got the afternoon off," Andy said.

"You have a job?" I asked. Too late, I tried to keep the astonishment out of my voice.

"Sure," he said. "What d'ya think, I rob banks to support my habit?"

"I knew a guy who robbed banks," Bud Porter said behind me.

I ignored him. "What do you do?" I asked Andy.

"Fix up furniture," he said. "I work with about a dozen second-hand shops in the area, fix up crappy stuff until it looks like something somebody'd want in their house. Makes me enough money to support the old addiction."

"You don't seem to have any problem with the old addiction."

"Why should I?" he asked. "If you're going to be addicted to something, you may as well be addicted to something that there's some possible payoff for in the end. Sure, I could smoke dope. But what good would that do me? Least this way I have a chance."

"A chance for what?"

"Winning," he said. "Like your mom. She could be drinking, you know. Or stuffing herself with doughnuts. You should be glad she's only buying lottery tickets. Gambling is the optimist's addiction. It's the only one that makes any sense."

"So why do you go to group if you don't care if you're addicted?"

"You know what I love about this town?" he asked, skirting

my question. "There's always the same number of people. I've been here my whole life and as many people as die or move out get born or move in. That always amazes me. Lots of little towns die, lots of towns boom. Not many towns are consistently thirty-five hundred people."

"You *like* that?"

"Good for my business," he said. "Somebody's always getting rid of furniture, but somebody's always looking to buy it. And all the stuff along the street on junk pick-up, you wonder where it's coming from. Attics. All the attics in this town are full. But they keep being full. I don't exactly understand it; I just ride with it." He took a drink from his Slurpee. "Whadda you do? You don't still live here, do you?"

"God, no," I said. "I live in Phoenix. I'll be going back soon."

"I knew a guy from Phoenix," Bud said from behind me. He lowered his magazine when I turned around. "He ate dirt."

"Wanna get some air?" Andy asked.

I was already standing. Andy said good-bye to Bud and we went back out onto the street.

"Old Bud," Andy said, heading back down Spruce. "He's got some stories. What's your story?"

"I don't have a story," I said. "Well, I do, but it's dull."

"I doubt that."

"Why?"

He shrugged. "Dunno," he said. "You just seem like someone with a story. You've got that aura about you."

"Give me a break," I said. "Your horses have auras?"

"Sure do," he said. "I'm just not so great at reading them most of the time."

We walked home. How many times had I walked this walk? Grade school, high school, girls beside me, boys beside me, no one beside me. It made me sick to think about; I could have closed my eyes and not missed a step.

"So what's in Phoenix?" Andy asked suddenly.

"My ex-husband's job," I said.

"I can see why you're so anxious to get back," he said. If I'd known him better, I probably would have hit him.

"Thanks for letting me buy you a Slurpee," he said.

"You're welcome."

"Maybe I'll see you around?"

"Maybe," I said. But I didn't really think so.

My mother was acting weird. Well, weirder. I'd walk into a room and catch her staring out the window. At the dinner table I'd offer her a cup of coffee three times before she'd even hear me. One morning she was in the shower for over an hour, and twice in the middle of the night I heard her above me, rummaging around in the attic. I wondered if she was up there looking for things she could sell.

The third time, I got out of bed and went up the attic stairs to find her. She was sitting on an old dining-room chair with a needlepoint pillow for a seat cushion. She had a box on her lap and was sifting through it.

"Whatcha looking at?" I asked.

She looked up, didn't seem surprised that I was standing there.

"Just things," she said. "Old Christmas cards, things like that."

"How come?"

She shrugged. "You're here," she said. "It's too sad for an old woman living alone to get up in the middle of the night to look through things in her attic. Makes it better if there's someone else in the house." She held up a construction-paper Santa Claus. "'Dear Mommy and Daddy,'" she read off the back. "'Ho, ho, ho, and I want some Hot Wheels. Love Teddy.'" She smiled. "He has a Camaro now."

"See, he got his Hot Wheels," I said. I rested my hand on an old TV. "Was this Daddy's?" I asked. "One of the things he was going to fix up?"

"Your father . . . ," she said. My whole life, this had been my mother's response to any mention of her first husband. "Your father . . . ," and nothing more. What else needed to be said?

"You gonna go to that group tomorrow?" I asked.

"I might," she said. "You have a message you want me to relay?"

"No," I said.

"He seems like a nice enough boy. Isn't often someone sits quietly in your front yard and waits to be acknowledged."

I was sleepy, and this pissed me off. "What are you saying, Mother? You think I should go on dates to the track with him? Make this gambling thing a real family affair?"

She was quiet. She set the box down at her feet. Then she said, "Honey, don't you ever just want to hope for something?"

"I think I've hoped enough, thanks," I said.

She gazed at the backs of her hands. "You know what Walt used to say about you? He used to say you were the best of the bunch. 'That girl,' he said, 'is going places.'"

"And here I am," I said. "In the attic in the middle of the night with my depressed mother, rooting through boxes of Christmas cards and petting broken-down TVs. Old Walt was a smart guy. I've really gone places, haven't I?"

"When are you leaving?" she asked wearily.

The question took me aback. "I don't know."

"Well figure it out," she said. "I was wrong about having someone else in the house. It's actually sadder when the other person is you, Kathy. Why don't you just pack your bags and go back to Phoenix? Better yet, why don't you get even further away? Would that make you happy?"

"Good night," I said.

"Will you be leaving tomorrow?"

"I can't leave tomorrow," I said. "Tomorrow you might win the lottery."

But she didn't. While she was at group I watched the drawing without her, went through all her tickets, and then left the pile sitting on the floor, wrote *Too Bad* on the top ticket, and went upstairs to my room. I lay in the dark and thought about what I would do when I got back to Phoenix. I pictured myself walking into my apartment and opening my mail, checking my answering machine. I saw myself changing into sweat pants and sitting down on the couch and flipping on the television, listening to the Mallorys next door fighting about whose turn it was to take the dog out.

I heard my mother come into the house. I thought she would come to my room, say good night, at least make some snide comment about the note I had left for her on her stack of loser tickets. But after the stairs creaked I heard her go into her room, then the sounds of the faucet, the flush of the toilet, and the soft din of the TV in her bedroom. Fine, I thought. And I closed my eyes.

In the middle of the night I was awakened by a noise. I sat up in bed and heard it again, hail pelting against my window. But it was only mid-September, no time for hail, even in stupid Illinois. I got up and went to the window, opened the blinds. Andy was standing on our front lawn, a handful of pebbles in his hand. He waved.

I closed the blinds, stood there motionless for a moment. Then I slipped on a loose sweatshirt, went downstairs, and opened the front door. He was sitting in the middle of the lawn, juggling the pebbles.

"What's up?" he said.

"What time is it?" I asked.

"I dunno," he said. "Three something."

I shivered against the cold and he stood up.

"Just back from your lucky track?" I asked.

He shrugged. "Not so lucky anymore."

"Didn't win the last race?"

"I didn't even make it to the last race."

A light came on in Mr. Jenkins's upstairs. I saw the blinds split, and I took a step back into the darkened doorway. Andy smiled.

"You gonna get busted? Think he might call your mom?"

"Police is more like it."

He shrugged. "No warrants on me," he said. "You want to walk?"

"Is the Sheetz open?"

"Open all night," he said. "But I'm busted. Wanna go down to the park?"

I looked up at Mr. Jenkins's window, and could see his shadow against the blinds. He was probably worried Andy was going to mess with his lawn.

"Okay," I said. "Let's go."

The park was four blocks away, where our street dead-ended. I had played there with my brothers as a child, spent years wading in the pond looking for gold until my oldest brother finally broke the news that I wouldn't find any.

"Saw your mom at group tonight," Andy said. "She's gonna be okay, you know? I think she'll stop pretty soon with the tickets. Sometimes people have weird ways of grieving."

"I guess," I said, unconvinced.

"She cracks me up, though. Spent half the meeting correcting the Brother's grammar."

"Why do you keep going?" I asked.

He shoved his hands in his pockets, shrugged. "I don't know," he said. "Good will, I guess. I take it wherever I can get it, and there's not much at the track."

"I'm going back to Phoenix," I said. "Tomorrow, probably."

He stopped. We were at the entrance of the park. On the banks of the small pond, dozens of ducks slept in groups of two and threes.

"How come?" he asked.

"My mother's had it with me."

"That's too bad," he said.

"Yeah?"

He started walking again. "I used to run in this park all the time," he said.

"What d'ya mean, run?"

"You know, run. Like walking, but faster. I did cross country in high school. I loved this place. Some of the guys always wanted to run on the track, around and around and around a thousand times. I always thought it was a lot nicer here."

"You were a Bee?"

He grinned. "I was more than a Bee. I was a District Champ Bee, 1984."

"No way," I said. "The sign. On the sign, that's you?"

"Me and five other guys, yeah."

I shook my head. "You're famous."

"Yep," he said. "That's me. Famous Andy of Carlisle. Ran the course in 16:55 thirteen years ago. Unforgettable, huh?"

"You still run?"

"Once in a while," he said. "At night, sometimes, when I go out the turnstile at the track, I just start sprinting to my car. Never much of a sprinter, but it feels good sometimes, to just turn on the gas."

He squatted down on the ground beside the pond. There were two ducks about twenty feet to our left, sound asleep beside each other, their beaks buried in their wings.

"Look at those guys," Andy said. "They're probably thankful there's no one pelting bread at them."

"I can't believe they're just sitting there," I said. "They usually get scared."

"They'll wake up in a minute," he said. "Pick up our scent or something, open their eyes and waddle away."

"How do you know?"

"I told you. I love this place."

I squatted down beside him.

"Hey, wanna wager?" he asked.

"On what?"

"I'll take the one on the right, the one with the brown in his feathers. He wakes up first, you buy me a Slurpee. The other one wakes up, you owe me nothing."

"Is that it?"

"What do you mean, is that it? A wager's a simple thing, Kathy."

"Okay," I said. "You're on."

I extended my hand and he took it. I tensed up for a second, almost lost my balance in my squat, and he gripped my fingers to keep me from falling.

"No cheating," he whispered. "You gotta stay still, or the bet's off."

So we sat there in silence, still holding hands, listening to the distant hum of the highway. There was no moon, and the water in the pond looked black and deep, reflectionless. My duck, the one on the left, fluttered a wing at a passing moth, seemed just on the verge of opening his eyes. I felt Andy's breath catch, and I thought of what my mother had said, about wanting to hope for something. A cool breeze from the west slid through the park; the leaves above us rustled and Andy's duck twitched his feathers in his sleep.

"Wake up," I whispered. "Wake up."

Stewart O'Nan

1964. My grandfather, Bart Smith, with his grandchildren—my brother John and my cousins Kathleen and Suzanne Vuillet (enjoying the popcorn). I'm the one in front, almost smiling.

Though most readers know him as one of *Granta's* Twenty Best Young American Novelists, Stewart O'Nan has long been a dedicated short-story reader and writer. In 1993 Tobias Wolff chose his first collection, *In the Walled City*, for the Drue Heinz Prize. Since then he has published *Snow Angels* (1994), *The Names of the Dead* (1996), *The Speed Queen* (1997), and *A World Away* (1998), all novels, while continuing to quietly write and publish stories.

STEWART O'NAN

Good Morning, Heartache

*H*e came to her because his mother was going through some hard times moneywise. Of course it was not money, really; there was a man who'd almost married her, a lost job, a car stolen from their parking lot. The schools, the neighborhood, even the weather seemed to play into the decision. Milwaukee was a city with no jobs, Yvonne said, and cold in winter, ice reaching into the grey lake. Maybe it was time to try Chicago (Miss Fisk didn't say it was the same lake, the same cold, the same city finally). Yvonne called her night after night, sometimes swearing bitterly, sometimes crying, and Miss Fisk could not say no.

He was ten when he came, a wick-thin boy with a high forehead and tiny ears. He had turn, a brisk way of saying "Ma'am" and "You're welcome" that she recognized as her own—a gift her daughter had passed on to him. He was a bright child, talkative, and quick to pick up on what she needed. He didn't cry when his mother got in the dented Chevy and drove away. At supper he ate everything on his plate and then asked if he could watch TV if he did the dishes. He wanted the bedroom next to hers, he said, and that first night how could she deny him?

Nothing changed. Maybe it was because she was a grand-

Glimmer Train Stories, Issue 33, Winter 2000
© 1999 Stewart O'Nan

mother, ready to give everything, nothing left to save up for. She flattered herself that he favored her; wasn't it plain in the slope of his forehead, the just-enough-to-whistle gap in his big front teeth? He knew when she needed to be alone and when she needed a little sugar. He could always get what he wanted from her, not like Yvonne. She wanted to think it wasn't weakness on her part, that she didn't give in to him just because he was a child. But didn't she secretly smile to herself in the kitchen, making corn-bread for him, thinking she'd been blessed? He was a gift she hadn't known she'd needed. He was hers.

He was her good boy. That's what she wanted to say when the police came, and then the one reporter from the *Courier*. Smart as day in school, too. She didn't know how he got mixed up in all that nonsense. But it wasn't completely true, no, not by that time—she'd found things in his closet, tucked deep in the toes of his winter boots—and so she told the reporter it was a shame, and that just last week he'd started a program at the Vo-Tech, he and Chris (the other boy, she said, so he'd know), the two of them together. Graphic design. He wanted to be an artist, she said, wondering if that really was true.

Yes, it was true, an artist. Why did she have to question everything now, as if his life with her had been false, had never happened?

There were people who needed his liver. The doctor said

there was nothing else they could do, so if she would just please go ahead and sign the papers they could begin the procedure. She needed to call her daughter, she said, and then there was no answer, the phone ringing in Milwaukee, in the new apartment she'd visited just once, marveling at the plush, just-vacuumed carpet, the frost-free refrigerator, the view of the freezing lake—marveling at Yvonne's hard-won success, after all her troubles. Benny only had another year in school, and he was on the honor roll again. It didn't make sense to take him away from his friends.

"Legally you *are* his guardian," the lady in the office reminded her, and turned the form so Miss Fisk could write on the line. It wasn't like he was alive and she was saying take him off the machine; he was already dead, the blood stopped, his body cooling. There was someone who would die if she didn't sign this; that's what it came down to. She was not a selfish woman, Lord knows. She would do anything to save another mother this pain. Then why did she have to call Yvonne again?

The woman turned her phone to Miss Fisk, and she punched in the number, then waited. She pictured the empty apartment and wondered where Yvonne had gone off to. The corner store with its Miller sign and its high-priced milk. She thought of her walking the dark streets, smoking her cigarettes one after another like when she was angry. Was it raining there too? The phone rang five, six times. She put the receiver down and looked at the woman. "You say we need to do this now."

He was ten when he came and seventeen when he was taken from her, but there was another time before that when he was a baby, her first grandchild. She'd flown to Minnesota to be with Yvonne when the time came. She wasn't in the room, but she was right outside, waiting with her third awful cup of coffee, reading the classified ads from a discarded *Star-*

Tribune as Herman stared out over the city. He was Yvonne's boyfriend, and Miss Fisk knew he wouldn't be around to see this child raised right. But there was nothing she could do about it, and every time she said something, Yvonne would stop calling. And he did leave, eventually. He was still in St. Paul, still doing something in radio (she never knew quite what it was that he did). He came to the funeral, bending to her, accepting her arms as he never had before, saying, "Bertice," sadly, as if there were no words.

And where were you, she wanted to say. Call yourself a father. You have no right to grieve over him—no right. Benny never liked you because he knew what you are, and that is a no-count man who will never come to nothing.

Instead, she held on to him, told him to take care of Yvonne, something he'd never done, and never would.

They laid him to rest beside her Sherman, in the plot they'd bought for Yvonne. It seemed strange, standing there as the motor lowered the box; it was the first time Sherman had met Benny. They were neighbors now, and she liked that idea. Sherman would have liked the boy, mostly. In fact, if Sherman had been around, none of this would have happened.

But it did, it had. She had to remind herself sometimes, warming Rashaan's formula, that Benny was not going to be home in a few hours. When Vanessa came by after work and thanked her and took Rashaan home, cooing to him, tickling his chin, the house went quiet, only the clinking of the radiators, and she remembered everything. She had to turn the radio on to stop it.

"Yes, ma'am," the woman said, "it's no good after twelve hours," and still Miss Fisk hesitated, didn't pick up the pen. There didn't seem to be anything wrong with him, just the bump on his head, a few scrapes. How many hours had it been—two, three?

Some days she escaped completely, reading to Rashaan on

the sofa, fixing his strained peas, but then he left and the night spread endlessly in front of her, the rotation of the earth—the entire universe—her enemy. After Sherman, after Yvonne left for college, she thought she'd learned how to be alone. Then Benny came and changed that, dragged her back into the world of the living. Now the opposite was happening. Dusk congealed in the trees, crows flew over. She walked from window to window, stood with a hand gathering back the drapes, peering out over Spofford as if expecting him to come home for supper, his boots muddy from the new busway. Once, suddenly waking up in the present, she saw some of the Coleman children eating ice cream on the sidewalk, pointing up at her; when she waved, they scattered as if she were a witch.

"The tissue is what's important," the doctor said when they called him in. "The individual cells can live for a time by themselves, but eventually without nourishment from the blood, they die."

Yes, Miss Fisk wanted to say, I understand, but can't I just call one more time?

Supper was the hardest. Rashaan was with Vanessa again, and she could hear the clock above the sink tick off the minutes. The news was always the same. Sometimes she didn't make anything, just reached into the fridge, lifted the tinfoil and picked at a cold chicken, a butt of ham. She'd found a frozen macaroni she liked, and two or three times a week she pre-heated the oven and slid the little pan in, actually thankful for such convenience. It was thick, the crust on top brown and crunchy, the cheese inside steaming and heavy, burning the roof of her mouth. She ate until it was all gone, and then, disgusted with herself (remembering the velvet bite of her mother's, the pride she took in her own), she scrubbed the little tin and stacked it with the rest under the sink, thinking she could use them for something. For what?

And then there was the TV, the book from the library, a long biography of Mrs. Roosevelt. Now that her life was almost over, Miss Fisk was interested in history, as if to appreciate what she'd been through. Vanessa was taking a course; she always wanted her to read about people like Ralph Bunche and Adam Clayton Powell. Miss Fisk couldn't explain: Mrs. Roosevelt meant more to her, especially back then. Adam Clayton Powell she didn't particularly care for, though she couldn't remember why.

It was her Sherman: he must have suspicioned him of using the people for his own good. Sherman didn't trust a one of them baby-kissers, not even Martin Robinson. Oh, he'd listen to them talk, he wasn't close-minded, but the smoother they were, the less he heard.

It had been hard for her after Sherman died, but she had come through that. When Yvonne asked if she thought of him every day, automatically she said yes. It was so long ago, but she couldn't say that. People forget. And she had. It was natural. But now she found herself thinking of both Benny *and* him, the two of them over in Homewood Cemetery, lying there while the grass knotted its roots around their boxes.

He would have a long scar where they plucked it out with their instruments. No, not a scar, the skin wouldn't heal. Under the suit Yvonne bought for him would be a zipper of stitches. But how could she say this to the lady without seeming crazy?

Outside a siren boloed over the housetops, a car ripped past. Last month she'd been broken into; someone kicked out the basement window and stole her mother's silver. The screen was bent, glass all over the washing machine. She knew Yvonne was afraid for her, living in such a big house all by herself, but Miss Fisk was used to it. The only thing that scared her was the furnace. She'd get into bed and listen for it clicking in, the radiators knocking. When it didn't, she wondered if a gust had knocked out the pilot light, the basement slowly filling with sweet-smelling gas. Her greatest fear was going to investigate, flipping on the light at the top of the stairs, and suddenly being engulfed by a fireball. For that reason she kept a flashlight slung over the doorknob, and when she went down to do laundry, even in the summer, she clicked it on and picked her way through the cool, mildewy darkness like a burglar, sniffing.

Now the furnace kicked in, and the radiator next to her bed gurgled. She closed Mrs. Roosevelt and set her on the night table and cut off the light, fixed her pillows just the way she wanted them. She could sleep, it wasn't like she stayed awake all night, but there were a few minutes at the end of the day, in the dark, when it seemed there was nothing to do but think about Benny, and then Sherman, and these were the hardest times for her. Sleep would be merciful. And it was, it was, just not quickly enough.

Rashaan was a help. He was something to look forward to. In the morning Vanessa would ring the bell and then come right in, carrying his diaper bag, the big red dinosaur he slept with, and Miss Fisk would be fine again. But now, here in the dark, she remembered Benny eating cereal at the sink before running off to school, or in his room with his headphones on, doing his homework, and she closed her eyes tightly, wishing it away. Not him, no, she never wanted him to leave her—just as she would always have Sherman—but she was tired, so tired, didn't he understand?

In the morning it all began again. Five, five-thirty, rising with the sun. Tuesday, then Wednesday. August, September. Making her poached egg and toast, she noticed she'd forgotten to change the calendar. She ate with the radio, and still it didn't stop her from falling.

"We'll need your consent before we can do anything," the

lady said, like she'd forgotten, and Miss Fisk picked up the pen and angled the paper so she could write her name. "Press hard," the lady said, "you're making three copies," and then when Miss Fisk sank back in the chair, the one gesture exhausting her, she had more forms. Miss Fisk signed these without reading them, her perfect signature—practiced diligently, a source of pride to her as a girl—degenerating into scribble, huge loops and slashes. What was the date again?

June he did her hedges for her, him and Chris, working without their shirts to impress the girls, blue bandanas rolled into headbands to stop the sweat. He cut the lawn with the old push mower, oiling it from the same little red can Sherman did, replacing it in the same spot in the garage. She made lemonade for them because he didn't like ice tea (another part of Yvonne in him), and then they drank it on the porch, watching the Colemans playing whatever crazy game they'd made up.

A week after the accident, Harold Tolbert came to the door and said he thought he might trim her bushes out front if that was all right. She didn't have to ask, just showed him where the clippers were, rolled open the garage door. She even made lemonade, and he was kind enough to sit there on the porch with her, sipping it slow.

"Chris says hello," he told her. "He really wanted to be there."

"Well," she said, "it's not like he had a choice in the matter," and she asked after him. A wheelchair—for life, the doctors said. She couldn't imagine it, a young man, and so she said she was sorry and to please send him her regards. They didn't get into Chris and Vanessa breaking up, or Rashaan, though it hung in the air a minute. They didn't talk about how Harold never much cared for Benny, thought it was all his fault, a bad influence on Chris. It was just mischief; neither of them was wild like Harold's older one, though folks said he'd gotten

Jesus in prison.

The ice in Harold's glass rattled, and they both stood up.

"If there's anything we can do," he said.

There was and there wasn't. He could come and rake the leaves and shovel her walk and dig the garden in spring, but really there wasn't a thing he could do. It was exactly like after Sherman, she thought. She'd been so selfish. She'd thought that Benny would last her the rest of her life.

The one question she had for the lady was selfish, in a way: Who would get his liver?

The lady shuffled through a file to one side.

Miss Fisk expected her to say it was privileged information. She was ready to tear up the papers. Give you my only grandson's liver and you tell me it's none of my business?

"A Richard Skoda," the lady said. "Age sixteen."

White boy, she thought. Figures.

The lady went on to tell Miss Fisk about the condition he was born with and how he'd been waiting since he was eight, but Miss Fisk was picturing the doctors lifting it out of Benny and fitting it into Richard Skoda, the white boy all better, laughing with his family, and Benny being rolled away under a sheet.

Was it wrong to think this way?

She knew she would get past it eventually. She knew it was just grief, a temporary weakness, a susceptibility to all the things that had gone wrong in her life. And she knew just as strongly that she would return to her life, just as she had after Sherman. It would take time, that was all. Vanessa helped, and Rashaan. Sometimes she thought it was unhealthy how much she loved to hold him in her arms, that it would spoil him later. "You know your Auntie Bertie loves you, you know that, little boy, don't you?" she said, and tickled him the way she'd tickled Benny so long ago, the way she'd cooed to Yvonne, wrapped safe in her arms. Her sorrow now made those times seem that much sweeter, and she was grateful, yes, truly she was. This hurt of hers would pass, become a memory, join with all of her other ones, and those were mostly, oh, overwhelmingly happy. In time she would be fine.

But until then she was powerless in the grip of this, paralyzed, and knowing it was little help and no real comfort. She made lunch for the two of them, turned on the noon news while she spooned up Rashaan's diced turkey and potatoes, his whipped beets. There was weather and then sports and then it was his nap time. She did the few dishes they used, draped the dishrag neatly over the faucet. In the living room, Mrs. Roosevelt waited, no longer the first lady, gallivanting around the world now, an ambassador of good will. One son had been killed in the war. They mentioned it just once, and Miss Fisk thought that was wrong. Did it really go away so easily? Wouldn't she—like herself—look up from some book she was reading and think of him? Wherever she was, wouldn't her son be with her?

She had called Yvonne twice that night, hoping she would be home so she could make the decision. She was Benny's mother. But she wasn't home, and Miss Fisk had signed, and they'd taken his liver and given it to Richard Skoda. She was afraid of explaining this to Yvonne, and when she finally did get through, she waited until there was a lull and she could hear Yvonne clicking her nails the way she did when she was distracted and trying to think.

"Baby," she said, "they asked me if Benny would want to help some other people."

She waited, but Yvonne just clicked, went mmm-hmm.

"They said his insides were fine."

"They wanted him to donate his organs," Yvonne said, making it plain.

"I said I'd have to talk to you."

"I think he'd want to help other people."

"Oh, good," Miss Fisk said. "Oh, thank goodness."

"What?" she came back fast. "*What?* You didn't say they could, did you?"

"Now wait a minute," Miss Fisk said, but it was too late for that, and she knew this would stand between them for the rest of her life, would live in Yvonne long after she was laid to rest next to her Sherman. But hadn't she done the right thing?

Yes, she would answer herself, those steamy afternoons when the fan only pushed the hot air around the living room. She folded her clothes, fresh from the line, the TV on low so as not to wake Rashaan. Outside, the Coleman children were running up and down the sidewalk with their dog, a big German shepherd named Joey. One of the boys had a ball, and every time he threw it, she was ready to hear the squeal of brakes, the thump of the dog's heavy head against the bumper.

There was nothing, just the shrieks of children playing, the occasional car. Calm, bright. Shadows on the lawn. A day like today he'd be playing baseball down at the park with Chris, the two of them dragging back when it got too dark, grass stains on their ashy knees. He'd apologize for missing supper, then gobble down seconds and go out again with a new shirt, and hang out on Chris's stoop and smoothtalk the girls.

She finished the laundry and put it away, then checked on Rashaan, still sleeping, curled around his dinosaur. She stood there looking at him in the heat, a bright square of sun on the carpet. Soon he'd be grown too, off to a life she'd never see, and that was good. Time kept them moving on, that was the way of the world.

It was when she had nothing to do that she got in trouble. Like a child. Like a willful boy. In this house she'd lived in so many years, she could not help but have memories. But why couldn't she choose the ones she wanted to visit with?

It was the phone there in the front hall she answered, maybe a week after it happened. The funeral was done with:

the expensive stone in place, Yvonne back in Milwaukee, Herman in Minnesota, Chris still in the hospital. When the phone rang it could have been anyone. Those phone people were always trying to sell her windows that saved energy.

"Hello," a white woman said, overly polite, "is this Mrs. Bertice Fisk?"

"This is she."

"This is Maxine Skoda, Richard Skoda's mother. I just wanted to call and thank you and express our condolences about your grandson. I just wanted you to know how much your Benjamin's gift means . . ." Her voice wavered, broke, and she began to cry. "What this means," she tried, but she couldn't stop.

"That's all right," Miss Fisk said. "I understand."

"I'm sorry, I know it must be so hard for you."

"It is." But you don't see me crying, do you? she wanted to say. And *my* boy's dead.

It was a brief conversation, and pleasant, but while Miss Fisk said she was glad she called, in truth it meant little to her. She did not know these people at all. Yes, she was pleased they'd taken the time to acknowledge her loss, and she was genuinely relieved that her son would live because of Benny, that the operation had been a success, but she could not let the woman's happiness and grief touch her. She *would* not let it. There was so little left she could call her own.

This house. Yvonne's calls every Sunday. Vanessa returning from work to pick up Rashaan. It was enough, along with her memories, to fill the seasons. Fall was almost on them, then winter. She'd have to get Harold to come over and turn her garden, hang the storm windows. Have to have him look at the furnace, clean the burners.

There was always something that needed taking care of. The fuzzy rug in the upstairs bath sorely needed a wash. Those old Ebonys in the cellar she'd been meaning to get rid of, and the green duffel bag with the stain. They could wait till spring, she supposed.

That was the kind of thing she needed to keep her eye on, not all this mooning over what was already done with. Drive you to distraction, sure.

She had everything she needed right here. Oprah was on in fifteen minutes, and she had to wake up Rashaan, get him dressed and looking good for Vanessa. She had to start thinking about supper.

Changing Rashaan, she found herself thinking of what his life would be like, how she wished she could see how he turned out. She thought of Richard Skoda. His mother never called back, and since Miss Fisk hadn't seen his name in the obituaries (she read them every day, still shocked to see people she knew), she supposed he was fine, that he would grow to be a man and marry and have children to carry on his blood. Not like her and Sherman. Benny was the end.

Was that why he was so precious?

No. It was those tiny ears, and the way he couldn't stop asking questions at supper. The birthday presents he drew for her. The birdhouse he made in woodshop. It was because he favored her so, because for all those years she had raised him like he was her boy, and he was, despite anything Yvonne might say. It was not a lie: he was her good boy.

"Who's my good boy?" she asked Rashaan, lowering her nose to his. "Who's my bestest, goodest little boy?"

Later, when Vanessa had come and gone, she went back into the living room. Oprah was over. It was suppertime. She looked in the fridge, then searched the freezer for a tin of macaroni and cheese. She struggled with the plastic wrap, lifted off the cardboard instructions, pre-heated the oven to four hundred. It would be dark in another hour, the world shrunk to a room, a light, the book she was reading.

Outside the Coleman children were squealing, running

Joey into a lather. She stood at the window, a hand gathering back the drapes. The dog knocked one of the littler girls over, and she sat on the sidewalk, bawling and cradling her hand. Miss Fisk thought she should go out and help, but in a minute the girl's brother came by and knelt down, examining her hand like a doctor.

And then Miss Fisk was on the porch—oh, years ago, when Benny had just come from Milwaukee. He'd been riding some other boy's bike and lost control, and his palms were torn raw. The scrapes were filled with grit and she had to take him in to the sink and scrub them with hot, soapy water. He screamed and wrenched back and she had to pin him against the counter with her body, grip his wrists hard under the running water as he struggled. "It's the only way," she said, trying not to be angry with him. When she was done, he looked up at her, trembling, tears leaking out his eyes as if he didn't understand how she could be so mean. "Oh, baby," she said. "I'm sorry. Come here." She went to her knees and held him then, saying she was sorry, that she loved him. Didn't he know that? He had to know that.

"Benny," she said. "Baby, please."

"I know that," he said, and she crushed him against her, grateful—oh yes, blessed—vowing that as long as he was with her, she would never let anything hurt him ever again.

KAREN SWENSON
Writer

Interview
by Susan McInnis

Karen Swenson is the author of five collections of poetry: her new and selected, A Daughter's Latitude, Copper Canyon Press, 1998; The Landlady in Bangkok, *chosen by Maxim Kumin for the National Poetry Prize, Copper Canyon Press, 1994;* A Sense of Direction, The Smith, 1989; East-West, Confluence Press, 1980; *and* An Attic of Ideals, Doubleday, 1972. *She is*

Karen Swenson

widely published in literary magazines and anthologies, and dispatches from her travels appear regularly in the New York Times, *the* New Leader, *and the* Wall Street Journal, *among other publications. Swenson holds a BA from Barnard College and an MA from New York University. She taught for fourteen years at City College of New York, Clark University, Skidmore College, and Scripps, and has been a working journalist since 1989. Swenson lives presently in Manhattan. She spends two months of every year traveling, frequently visiting Burma, Indonesia, Malaysia, Thailand, Vietnam, Cambodia, and Tibet.*

Glimmer Train Stories, Issue 33, Winter 2000
© *1999 Susan McInnis*

Travel is a vital thread in life and work for you. What has made you a traveler, rather than a woman who takes vacations?

I come from traveling women. In 1930, my mother did something odd for a nice, well-bred young lady from Fargo, North Dakota. She took a friend with her to Europe. Once there, she quickly talked this woman into traveling with her from Paris down to southern France, then on to Sicily, and from there onto a boat bound for Tunisia. A few weeks after they landed in Tunis, my mother convinced her companion to go home. She stayed on, and spent four months alone in Tunis. Neither Sicily nor Tunis were exactly "travel destinations" in 1930, and certainly not for young women on their own. So it was a bold step.

She never urged me to follow her lead. There was never any "You *must* go to North Africa," but she communicated clearly that, although going to see the world's museums and its lovely places was part of travel, essentially travel has to do with adventure. It has to do with being in an alien environment, and with taking risks. She never said any of this outright, but the message was clearly there.

Adventure, risk taking, and alien lands could be frightening to some people. To you it was a siren song.

Yes, it was a siren, definitely. And, yes, I do understand how one could be frightened. I don't mean to say that I'm not terrified when I take risks. I frequently end up in the middle of something thinking, "What is the matter with me? Why am I doing this to myself? This is *not* necessary." But the lure is always there. And it definitely comes through my mother, although in other aspects of her life she was not particularly given to taking risks.

Your first solo journey was to Thailand, which seems like a leap off the high dive for a beginning traveler. Was it?

Actually, I hedged my bets. I went to Nepal first, with a group, to make sure I could cope alone. That was what hooked me. After I'd gone to Nepal, there was no doubt in my mind that this was the part of the world for me, and going to Thailand was just what I should do next. I knew the kind of travel I envisioned would be very difficult, but I can still remember myself standing in the middle of Nepal, saying, "You can do this. You can do it alone. This is *not* impossible."

So I left Nepal, went home, saved my money, and in a couple of years I had enough to go to Thailand on my own. The choice of Thailand was also partly inspired by my mother. She had taken a trip around the world in 1961, and when she came back, I asked her what was best. She said Thailand—there was nothing like it. So I headed there. And I *was* scared. Sufficiently so that I couldn't do what I wanted to do. I had planned ahead, read my guidebooks, and knew I wanted to stay in Thailand's little guest houses. They're extremely cheap, so they free up a lot of money, making it possible to travel longer and farther. But I couldn't do it. I got into Bangkok and headed straight for an American-style hotel. It was relatively inexpensive by our standards—thirty-five dollars a night. But I felt terribly ashamed about my lapse of nerve.

As it turned out, the country forced me to take the risk I couldn't take on my own. As I traveled away from Bangkok, I got into smaller and more remote places where it was harder and harder to find "American" hotels. Finally on a bus one day, I made friends with a man who was kind enough to point out guest houses when we came to Sukhothai. And of course, once I actually spent the night in a guest house, I realized it was perfectly okay. There were no bed bugs. There were no fleas. Whatever terrified me wasn't there. There was a crummy bathroom, but it was my bathroom, which was not always the case.

When I first arrived in Bangkok, I'd seen a little alley across from my hotel, and there were two guest houses there, both mentioned in my travel guides. One was the Suneeporn Guest

House. I went there when I returned from that first trip into the country, armed with new courage, and found that the landlady was a woman about my age. She was used to having "young things" come to stay in her guest house, and looked at me with great curiosity. And I was equally curious about her. Since then I've generally stayed at the Suneeporn whenever I've been in Bangkok.

Is she the landlady of "The Landlady in Bangkok"?

Yes. That poem emerged in part from the language barrier between us. She speaks rudimentary English, but I don't speak much Thai at all. Thai's a terrifying language. For one thing, it's spoken in five tones, so if you're not fluent you can make errors that just are beyond belief.

With more than basic communication largely blocked, those of us who stay at the Suneeporn really don't know anything about our landlady. We invent her, as the poem says, "Because, separated from us by a language / We find her a character without a plot." We invent a husband for her, "graft invention on observation ... She has no history for our words of home / As we've no history for the weal of scar / Raised on her shoulder."

The landlady of the poem frees caged sparrows at the temple. In Thailand, you buy a cage of sparrows, climb the temple steps, and open the cage to free them. Buddhist teachings say you gain merit any time you free something that is caged. But, of course, the act is also symbolic. You are giving the sparrows what you hope will happen to you: that you will break the cycle of reincarnation—Samsara—and be freed into Nirvana where you never have to be reincarnated, never have to live life again. It's basic to Buddhism that in life you do it until you get it right.

The poems in this collection, The Landlady in Bangkok, *are about the particulars of life in Southeast Asia, but they also transcend land and culture, and shrink the distance between West and East.*

What part do the universals you explore play in your thinking and writing?

I think that inclination to see the universal has been automatic with me, though I didn't really set out to do it. It just became apparent as I traveled that, underneath a certain glaze, a certain veneer of culture, we are very, very similar.

You write that the veneer separates us, keeps us from recognizing our common humanity, and that culture, at its worst, breeds what you call an "evilness that is only human."

That we all share, and all try to dodge.

Can you explain? You confront it in "We," among other poems.

"We" is about a museum in Saigon. Since the U.S. reestablished relations with Vietnam, there have been suggestions that it be closed, which I think would not be a good idea. It should stay open. It's a Vietnamese war museum, of course, so the exhibits show what the Americans did to Vietnamese during the war, and what the Khmer Rouge did to them. It doesn't examine what the Vietnamese did to their enemies.

In the poem, "One pronoun keeps at bay our guilt: / They, they, they..." The heartless one, you say, like the enemy, is always the "other."

And that means the poem is not just about us, about "We," but about *I*, too, our tendency to deny that each of us will torture, will kill, will maim, out of fear. Fear is the driving force, always. People who are sufficiently afraid will do things they couldn't otherwise imagine possible. In Vietnam, as anywhere, the "other" was dehumanized, making it possible for individuals to do unthinkable things to other human beings.

Even a museum as moving and disturbing as Washington's Holocaust Museum keeps visitors a reassuring step removed from the self, doesn't it? Because it examines "them," not us, not what we might do.

Yes, and we need to confront that potential in ourselves. Without that excruciating, unwilling step, we really can't change anything. Saying we must do something about "them," is far, far safer than realizing we've got to do something about "us," or about "me." This is true of cultural atrocities, but equally true closest to home, where there are battered women and battered children. It's all part and parcel of the same problem: what we do to each other.

Did your sense of what we all hold in common precede or grow out of your travels?

Both, I suppose. I think I suspected the common thread. But it really began to come clear to me once I was out there, traveling and talking to people who live under very different conditions than I'd ever known. One of the reasons I like Thai society so much is that women flow freely in a culture that is otherwise extremely stratified. They're interested in each other, and they talk with each other, from the poorest women to the wealthiest aristocrats. There's a lively exchange between them, a mutual attraction, and they're also very interested in women from outside their culture. I remember on a visit to the ruins at Phimai, a woman came up to me and said, "You speak Thai?" I said no and apologized, and she said, "I no speak English. This very bad. I want talk to you." She was most interested in this woman who was so different, but still related in some significant way.

Your writing life was encouraged by your mother, by a high-school teacher, and also rather provocatively by a husband. He said something like, "You're never going to write. You'll talk about it forever, but you'll never do it." A challenge?

Definitely. I've always had a tendency to take dares, and I react fairly violently to challenges, especially from the male of the species. I fell out of a tree when I was about eight. It was a pretty drastic fall, about twenty feet onto rocks, and my family thought I'd ruptured my spleen. It was all because a little boy said, "You can't stand on that branch!" And I said, "Oh, yes I can!"

Much later, my then-husband issued his challenge. It took

me a long time to realize he was probably challenging himself, as much as me. He also wanted to write, and later did some wonderful columns for *Cycle* magazine about cycling around the United States. But at the time I took his disgust very personally—and thank heaven! It set me right on the path. He was right. I was just talking. I wasn't writing.

You were married, had a child, were not traveling, and not writing. Was this a period of percolation for you?

Well, at the time I was convinced I was lazy. It's not true, but I would have mistaken mulling and percolation for laziness then. And indeed, I'd gained just barely enough life experience to start writing about something other than myself, to move a few steps out into the world in my writing. So it was a good time to start. I was twenty-five.

How old was your son?

He was an infant. I put him in a little seat I could rock with my foot so he'd be quiet while I was writing. That went on for years. When he was nine, he protested. "Everybody else in my class stays up until nine or ten o'clock," he said. "How come I go to bed at 6:30?" And I said, "Because your mother writes." We made a deal. He could stay up, but he couldn't interrupt me unless he was bleeding to death or the house was on fire. I emerged at 9:30 or 10 every night, gave him a kiss, and tucked him in.

And I assume he grew up to be a healthy human being?

I honestly have no idea whether he's a healthy human being. I don't think parents can judge that. But it worked. I got my time to write and it was fine.

In looking at what has influenced both travel and writing for you, an early event, a death when you were still a child, seems pivotal. What happened?

I grew up on what was then called a private road. It had been an estate, but the main mansion burned down, the estate owner moved on, and other people bought the remaining quarters. My family lived in the dairy barn, and there was another family with a number of children up at the chapel. Their little boy, Billy Bliss, was half a year older than I, and we spent all our time together. We were absolutely best friends. I was very bossy and he'd get thoroughly annoyed with me, and he'd do boy things I absolutely loathed—snow down my neck and things like that—but we were inseparable.

Then when I was eleven, I was out in Fargo with my great aunts, and a letter arrived from Billy's mother saying he was dead from pneumonia following appendicitis. I didn't cry. I can remember my mother watching me to see what I was feeling, but the very idea that Billy might die was incomprehensible to me. I was in shock.

After I got back, on the first day of school, I walked down to the edge of the driveway and just stood there, waiting. Billy's older brother came along and took me the rest of the way. We didn't talk about Billy, although he was clearly there between us. After school I must have put it all together. I walked home alone, thinking, "Okay, Billy is dead, and I have a life and Billy didn't get his. So I have to live for both of us, and I have to make a good enough life so that he doesn't lose out."

I suppose that's another explanation for my traveling, although I can't travel as Billy. I have to travel as Karen, and in some ways traveling as a woman is not as good as traveling as a man. There are advantages, like the connections you make with other women. But the downside is there, too. I think of the brothers, Lawrence and Lorne Blair, who wrote *The Ring of Fire: An Indonesian Odyssey*, and who've done everything you've ever wanted to do in life. Many of the images in "What Does a Woman Want," —the title, of course, comes from our Mr. Freud—come from *The Ring of Fire*.

It's a swashbuckling poem. The boys go off to "munch sago grubs with cannibals," to sailing ships and volcanoes and feats of derring-do. But you certainly don't stay at home with your needlework. If you're

envious of the male freedom, you're still out there adventuring full-
speed ahead, as the poem says: "sails spread ... before the salty wind."
Well, you've got to. You can't shrink. Think about what the
everyday discouragements do to you! Consider what's implied
when people say, "Aren't you afraid to travel alone?" When I
first heard that, I thought, "What a peculiar question!" I can
understand you'd be afraid to travel in certain places, but
people asked me that when I was still traveling around the
United States with a cat, sleeping in the back of a Honda
hatchback. I'd be putting in the wash at a laundromat, and
some woman would say, "You're traveling alone? Oh! I
wouldn't do that!"

And then one day it hit me that the warnings and incredu-
lity are all about rape. And while I would never minimize the
issue or the danger, in ten years of traveling in Southeast Asia
two months out of every year, only once have I experienced
anything close to it. I was in an extremely isolated situation
with a boy and two men. I think the men simply assumed that
the reason I was abroad alone was because I needed to get laid.
One guy grabbed me. I screamed. And in that moment I saw
his face change. He was horrified! As horrified as any Western
man who'd spilled a bowl of hot soup down somebody's
décolletage. He had committed the ultimate social solecism
and he was aghast.

He ran. Not because he was afraid of being caught. If he had
really been intent on rape, there wasn't a thing keeping him
from it. I frankly think he had seen too much Madonna, too
much of the Western porn that comes out of Hong Kong. The
videos and movies directly affected what he saw when he
looked at me. When I go to a French movie, I assume I am
seeing the French more or less as they are, and he wasn't seeing
porn cartoons on the screen. He was seeing real men and
women. What was he supposed to think?

That's the worst I've faced, and it would never keep me from traveling. What I have is too good to give up.

Do you see links over time, between your freedom to choose travel and writing—even if your choices fly ahead of warnings and discouragements—and the culture opening up to more possibilities for women?

If the society is dominated by an "other" who thinks differently than you do—whether you're woman, black, Asian, or Eskimo—you tend to deny your own thoughts and your own possibilities. But if the domination begins to break down, to make room for other possibilities, then what's been hidden or denied begins to percolate up. People begin to think their own thoughts, and to listen to what they're thinking, and the culture opens up to them, becomes interested in the new voices, begins to see itself differently because of them. The culture becomes more complex, more interesting.

What is true for a culture is true for poetry?

Absolutely. At some point it occurred to me that in reading the first thousand years of poetry, I'd never came across a poem about childbirth. There aren't even any children in *Beowulf*. They sit at a table somewhere, but they aren't part of the story. Nor are there children in Chaucer. There are women, important women in Chaucer, whereas the women of *Beowulf* are shadows. And then, Shakespeare, that very peculiar man, was a feminist. There's just not a moment's doubt about it, although why it should have been true, one can't imagine. But you can feel the tide shift. The world of thought and possibility begins to open up.

Do you see changes such as these as evolutionary, that the various cultures of the world will progressively open to their diverse influences?

It's not possible to generalize. Our culture has changed, but I don't know if it's evolution or an aberration spurred by economic progress. And cultural roots are so idiosyncratic. In matriarchal India, for example, men's thoughts and ideas and feelings have been quashed. People say fairly horrifying things, like, "Everyone knows who the mother of a child is. Who the father is is a matter of conjecture." Such an unpleasant little phrase.

So each side can take advantage of the other. It's a convention I write about in "Getting a Purchase," about a young Canadian college student who "rents" a Thai woman for a month, to be his interpreter, guide, and sexual companion. She was sold to a bar by her farmer father, along with her sister, when the family fell on hard times, and now must tolerate being rented out to others. In this case, the student who rents her isn't particularly unkind to her, but nor does he seriously consider what he's doing.

"Getting a Purchase" is one of a number of profiles in The Landlady in Bangkok.

Yes. I hope they become meditations for readers, springboards for reflection and consideration. There's one about an Irish man who is gay. He's found that attitudes about homosexuality in Thailand have allowed him to make an extraordinary life for himself there. It seemed to me that his story was very important, as was the story about the young man who hired a woman. What was he thinking? That you buy a woman for a month? How do you decide that's all right? In both cases, the subjects needed to be discussed. There is another story that I haven't written yet, because I don't know the woman well enough. She's trapped by loan sharks, and to dig herself out of that situation, has become the head of a Bangkok whorehouse.

You need to know a great deal about people to write about them, much more than you actually put into the work. You must understand the facts, but much more importantly, the feeling of the person. In the case of the student, I traveled with him and with his hired companion, and the gay man is probably one of my three best friends in Thailand. You build up a great deal of background knowledge, watching and listening, living and traveling with people. The writing is a process of selecting and leaving out, and sometimes inventing—since poems aren't the absolute truth. They're more like epitomes.

Have you written about life and people in New York as you do about Southeast Asia?

I haven't, really. I have poems that have come out of New York, but not a collection as yet. As I travel back and forth, though, I see that New York is another place where you can get lost and find your own thread at the same time.

What's lost and what's found for you as you travel away from New York?

When you travel, you lose your societal roles. You are no longer enclosed. The shell just drops off. Of course, you aren't totally free. You acquire constraints in the other culture, but they don't really inhibit you much. And you might smack into a cultural wall once in a while, but, still, you *think* you're free, and that's what's important. We talked earlier about my mother, and my sense that I come from traveling women. I am sure my mother felt imprisoned by the cultural roles available to her. Traveling for her was a way out, and I am sure it is a way out for me, too.

I have used travel to break through constraining roles, but also to work on fear. Women of my generation and culture were taught to be afraid. It was "appropriate" to be afraid then. Timid women were thought to be appealing women. Men felt braver around them, and the timid woman was more likely to get a husband, among other perquisites.

But on reflection, it's clear that when you put on that mask, it adheres to your face. It must be worked off. For me, going to strange places was a way of working the mask off. Southeast Asia. Nepal. Tibet.

If you were to describe those countries in a word, what would it be?
Comfortable.

What makes them comfortable?

Buddhism. I'm not a Buddhist, and don't ever expect to be, although I've picked up some very useful things from Buddhism. But I find Buddhist countries lovely places to be in. The people behave in ways I find understandable. I have to watch my manners because they are much more mannerly than Westerners. But I find their way of life and their way of seeing life very comfortable, very open. It opens things for you. Definitely.

Susan McInnis is a producer for public radio, a writer, and an editor living in Fairbanks, Alaska. Her interviews with Toi Derricotte, Alberto Ríos, and Patricia Hampl have appeared in *Glimmer Train Stories*. Interviews with Antonya Nelson and Lee Smith have appeared in *AWP Chronicle*.

The Last Pages

Grace Elizabeth Throckmorten, two years old

*A*gain, my grandfather, Bart Smith. My mother gave me this picture years ago, so the pose is familiar, etched in memory. Here's the light coming through the window, burning the film inside the camera white. There's the blur of his left hand, checking his pocket watch, sometime in the fifties.

All his life, Poe carried a tiny portrait of his mother, who died when he was three; set it by his bed wherever he slept. In Philadelphia, Randy Rosensteel, the special collections curator, showed me the portrait. Eliza Poe was an actress known for her singing, and in the portrait her beauty is exaggerrated, her eyes impossibly large. Though I didn't know her, I could feel the weight and complexity of Poe's history with her, something, as a writer, I have to draw upon for all of my people.

When I look at Grandpa Smith, he reminds me of the breadth of emotion and experience we all carry within us. With Miss Fisk, I had to come to know her history and then show just a fraction of it, hint at the vastness of her life. But that part was easy. It was already there.

GEORGE MANNER

I was especially glad when *Glimmer Train* informed me I'd won their Poetry Open because I've always had a particular fondness for this poem. Even though it has been several years since I wrote it, I still remember the feeling I had at my table—that, upon finishing the last stanza, I was somewhere new and old.

It is one of only two dramatic monologues I've written. Perhaps the persona poem is one of the things I'm heading toward; I don't know, but that'd be fine with me.

Here I am with my two children, Emily and Bret.

Thanks, *Glimmer Train*.

I wrote "Cosgrove's Dilemma" several months after my husband and I visited Ireland, but the idea must have taken root in my unconscious atop a boggy, wind-swept hill in Connemara, where, with each step on the spongy earth, I sensed I was approaching my perceived destiny of death by suffocation in a murky bog. In a Dublin bookstore I had come across Bram Stoker's first novel, *The Snake's Pass*, which takes place in Connemara and features a quaking bog, a geological feature probably no longer a threat to hill walkers in Ireland; but this phenomenon piqued my imagination, generating overwhelming terror. I must have combined this fear with my fear of being swallowed by suburbia, for I *am* Herbert Cosgrove, right down to the unkempt lawn; and being true Winicks, my husband and two daughters also refuse to maintain an attractive lawn and porch without mildew and peeling paint, though at times we ruminate on what it would be like to have a lovely English garden and perhaps a maze of sculpted bushes, too, if just one of us enjoyed gardening.

MANUEL MUÑOZ

$\mathcal{C}$ampo" is based in my home-town of Dinuba, California, a farming community of about fifteen thousand right in the middle of the Central Valley. The stories I'm working on now are set there as well, though I've chosen not to call it Dinuba (or anything else). Naming and renaming is one of the liberties I've not been able to take, though I have been doing so with everything else, mostly as a way to worm out of writing that is too autobiographical. Home is no longer the way I remember it and, having lived on the East Coast since college, I'm more willing to reinvent the place, the people in it.

This story created all sorts of problems for me. Even now, I feel it is unresolved, that these women in the poppy dresses and the farmworker boys need to reappear elsewhere, unnamed as they are. These bright orange flowers took a while to get out of my system—I think the finding of the boys' names will take a lot longer, that some time needs to pass before I can invent that moment, how boys come to name themselves.

JAMES CARLOS BLAKE

*A*lthough I spent my early boyhood in Mexico and Texas, I have lived much of my life in the American South, and that culture has shaped my sensibilities and writing interests as much as any other.

"Old Boys" deals with a breed of men I know well and have always held in high affection, a naturally dramatic type given to chronic misadventure, spectacular marital conflict, relentless mystification about the women they revere, abiding delight in the natural world, and a characteristic penchant for telling stories of it all. What's more, the women of that world can give as good as they get, making every romance, every marriage, the stuff of good stories, many of them funny, most of them rooted in love.

I dread having to write about my own work; I almost never have an interesting tale to tell about a story's genesis. When people ask me where I get my ideas I try my best to change the subject. If pressed, I usually come out with something like, "Um, I make them up?" Thus, what follows is a list of some of my favorite things that do not appear in, nor in any way inspired, "The Greater Grace of Carlisle."

Ballpark:	Busch Stadium
Billy Joel song:	"Summer, Highland Falls"
Card game:	Spades
Chapter:	7, *All the King's Men*
Condiment:	Gravy
Dog toy:	Daily Growl
First Lady:	Barbara Bush (because she broke her arm sledding)
Movie scene:	Poker on the train, in *The Sting*
Shirt:	The one my mother says looks like Grandpa Broeder's bathrobe (not a compliment)
Yankee:	Lou Gehrig

MARGO RABB

*T*he character of Kelsey is loosely based on my best friend, Julien Yoo (she's the one on the right). We met our freshman year in high school, and have been friends for fourteen years. Recently, we spent the afternoon at the Whitney Museum in Manhattan, and as we giggled our way from exhibit to exhibit, a guard asked us, seriously, "Are you two sisters?"

I think, in so many ways, we are.

ROLAND SODOWSKY

*H*aving lived in some very dissimilar environments—a crowded industrial neighborhood in Germany, an adobe house in West Texas, a rundown compound in West Africa, among others—I'm fascinated by the human ability to adapt, which is the subject of my story, "What We Have to, What We Can." As I wrote the story, I felt it was developing as an optimistic statement about our ability to move on, to change, to try to be happy. I hope it turned out that way.

$\mathcal{P}$AST CONTRIBUTING AUTHORS AND ARTISTS
Issues 1 through 32 are available for eleven dollars each.

Robert A. Abel • Linsey Abrams • Steve Adams • Susan Alenick • Rosemary Altea • Julia Alvarez • A. Manette Ansay • Margaret Atwood • Kevin Bacon • Aida Baker • Russell Banks • Brad Barkley • Kyle Ann Bates • Richard Bausch • Robert Bausch • Charles Baxter • Ann Beattie • Barbara Bechtold • Cathie Beck • Janet Belding • Sallie Bingham • Kristen Birchett • Melanie Bishop • Corinne Demas Bliss • Valerie Block • Joan Bohorfoush • Harold Brodkey • Danit Brown • Kurt McGinnis Brown • Paul Brownfield • Judy Budnitz • Evan Burton • Michael Byers • Christine Byl • Gerard Byrne • Jack Cady • Annie Callan • Kevin Canty • Peter Carey • Brian Champeau • Mike Chasar • Robert Chibka • Carolyn Chute • George Clark • Dennis Clemmens • Robert Cohen • Evan S. Connell • Ellen Cooney • Wendy Counsil • Toi Derricotte • Janet Desaulniers • Tiziana di Marina • Junot Díaz • Stephen Dixon • Michael Dorris • Siobhan Dowd • Eugenie Doyle • Andre Dubus • Andre Dubus III • Wayne Dyer • Barbara Eiswerth • Mary Ellis • Susan Engberg • Lin Enger • James English • Tony Eprile • Louise Erdrich • Zoë Evamy • Nomi Eve • Edward Falco • Lisa Fetchko • Michael Frank • Pete Fromm • Daniel Gabriel • Ernest Gaines • Tess Gallagher • Louis Gallo • Kent Gardien • Ellen Gilchrist • Mary Gordon • Peter Gordon • Elizabeth Graver • Gail Greiner • John Griesemer • Paul Griner • Patricia Hampl • Christian Hansen • Elizabeth Logan Harris • Marina Harris • Erin Hart • Daniel Hayes • David Haynes • Daniel Hecht • Ursula Hegi • Amy Hempel • Andee Hochman • Alice Hoffman • Jack Holland • Noy Holland • Lucy Honig • Ann Hood • Linda Hornbuckle • David Huddle • Stewart David Ikeda • Lawson Fusao Inada • Elizabeth Inness-Brown • Andrea Jeyaveeran • Charles Johnson • Wayne Johnson • Thom Jones • Cyril Jones-Kellet • Elizabeth Judd • Jiri Kajanë • Hester Kaplan • Wayne Karlin • Andrea King Kelly • Thomas E. Kennedy • Jamaica Kincaid • Lily King • Maina wa Kinyatti • Carolyn Kizer • Carrie Knowles • Jake Kreilkamp • Marilyn Krysl • Frances Kuffel • Anatoly Kurchatkin • Victoria Lancelotta • Jennifer Levasseur • Doug Lawson • Don Lee • Peter Lefcourt • Jon Leon • Doris Lessing • Debra Levy • Janice Levy • Christine Liotta • Rosina Lippi-Green • David Long • Salvatore Diego Lopez • Melissa Lowver • William Luvaas • Richard Lyons • Bruce Machart • Jeff MacNelly • R. Kevin Maler • Jana Martin • Lee Martin • Alice Mattison • Jane McCafferty • Cammie McGovern • Eileen McGuire • Susan McInnis • Gregory McNamee • Jenny Drake McPhee • Frank Michel • Nancy Middleton • Alyce Miller • Katherine Min • Mary McGarry Morris • Mary Morrissy • Bernard Mulligan • Abdelrahman Munif • Kent Nelson • Sigrid Nunez • Joyce Carol Oates • Tim O'Brien • Vana O'Brien • Mary O'Dell • Chris Offutt • Laura Oliver • Elizabeth Oness • Karen Outen • Mary Overton • Patricia Page • Peter Parsons • Constance Pierce • Steven Polansky • Jessica Printz • Annie Proulx • Kevin Rabalais • Jonathan Raban • George Rabasa • Paul Rawlins • Nancy Reisman • Linda Reynolds • Anne Rice • Alberto Ríos • Roxana Robinson • Paulette Roeske • Stan Rogal • Frank Ronan • Elizabeth Rosen • Janice Rosenberg • Jane Rosenzweig • Karen Sagstetter • Kiran Kaur Saini • Libby Schmais • Natalie Schoen • Jim Schumock • Lynn Sharon Schwartz • Barbara Scot • Amy Selwyn • Catherine Seto • Bob Shacochis • Evelyn Sharenov • Ami Silber • Floyd Skloot • Gregory Spatz • Brent Spencer • Lara Stapleton • Barbara Stevens • George Stolz • William Styron • Liz Szabla • Paul Theroux • Abigail Thomas • Randolph Thomas • Joyce Thompson • Patrick Tierney • Andrew Toos • Patricia Traxler • Rob Trucks • Kathryn Trueblood • Carol Turner • Christine Turner • Kathleen Tyau • Michael Upchurch • A.J. Verdelle • Daniel Villasenor • Daniel Wallace • Ren Wanding • Mary Yukari Waters • Jamie Weisman • Lance Weller • Ed Weyhing • Joan Wickersham • Lex Williford • Gary Wilson • Terry Wolverton • Monica Wood • Christopher Woods • Celia Wren • Calvin Wright • Brennen Wysong • Jane Zwinger

1942

Coming soon:

"It's not that I'm closed to this," I say, and feel an uncharacteristic wave of confession overtaking me. "I always thought I'd probably have kids. I mean, I still see it as a possibility. It's just rather indistinguishable from wanting a trip to Brazil, or swimming lessons, or a million other things."

from "Beneath the Earth of Her" by Karen E. Outen

We go in my newly convertible Dodge Dart. What I should say is newly converted, because really, there's no getting back to how it was.

from "Getting the Dog" by Felicia Olivera

People parked their cars in these concrete carports that had little wooden cabinets for locking up all the junk you're never going to need, but, for one reason or another, can't afford to part with.

from "Something for Nothing" by William J. Cyr

When I wrote my novel *Rebel Powers*, there wasn't any aspect of the writing that wasn't fun, that I didn't look forward to in the mornings. I never used an alarm clock. I would wake up at sunlight. There was a big shadow of the house on the lawn, and I would know that by the time I was through with that day's work, the shadow would be on the other side of the house. It was a wonderful time.

from an interview with Richard Bausch
by Jennifer Levasseur and Kevin Rabalais